CW01083636

Malachi's Wish

&

Yours, Milo

The Four Corners Series

JS Grey

This book was published thanks to free support and training from:

TCKPublishing.com

<u>TRIGGER WARNINGS</u>

Whilst every effort has been made to deal with delicate situations respectfully and with compassion, certain scenes in this short story may be considered triggering for some people as the themes deal with homophobia, trauma, and physical assault. We hope that you read this story with an open mind and read it in the way that it was intended.

Malachi's Wish story takes place before and after the events of Consuming Redemption. This short story can be read as a standalone, but further details are explained within the full-length novel.

Malachi's Wish

CHAPTER 1.

Ten Years Ago

Northern Ireland

The kitchen door swings open, the blustery wind from outside sweeping through the kitchen. The ruffles from the ivory white tablecloth on the round dining room table billow in the wind like we're in the set of a 1980's music video. My dad stands on the mat, dirty boots in hand as he shakes himself off like a wet dog.

"Would you close the fecking door!" my mother shrieks, standing in the doorway of the kitchen leading in from the living room where she has been knitting a shawl for old Pat's granddaughter down the street. She clutches the ball of wool tight in her hand as she runs the other up and down her arm to ward away the goosebumps.

"Yeah Pa, you're letting all the heat out," my sister Dawn whines from behind me. I turn to see her pressing her knees together, shoulders hunched over as she stirs a large pot on the stove with a giant wooden ladle. The air in the kitchen is thick with the deliciously warm smell of the vegetable stew my sister has been preparing for the past hour.

"Oh, I'm sorry Princess," my dad bellows from the back door, "you're more than welcome to come down to the barn and help the hands with the sheep; they've helped deliver fifteen lambs this evening. They are down there right now, covered in blood. You can go on down, and I'll stir your soup for you?" Gentle mirth plays on his face.

"Fifteen?" my mother gasps. "Are the farmhands switching over with the night shift soon?" Taking a seat at the table next to me, my mother continues with her knitting.

"Yes, I'm just coming up for a break and then I'll go back down before the shift change, most of the other girls down there only had one or two labs, Old Lindy though had three. She looks a little worse for wear so I'm going to sit with her awhile I think." Closing the door behind him, my dad places his boots on the coarse brown mat in the mudroom before shucking off his rainproofs and hanging them up on the metal hooks behind the door. "When did you get back up here boy?"

"About twenty minutes ago Pa," I call from behind a large mug of coffee, warming my hands. "I helped Misty deliver her first lamb, she caught me off guard so I had no chance to put my gloves on. My hands were not a pretty sight after."

My dad chuckles, walking around the table and pats me on the shoulder. "I'd imagine not boy, no." Taking his spot at the head of the table, he rests his large hands on the top and drums his fingers against the tablecloth. "I was surprised you came home to help with the lambing, to be honest Niall, thought maybe being in that fancy university in Dublin might have softened you up boy."

My mother rests her head softly against my shoulder and laughs lightly.

"Are you kidding," Dawn says, coming up behind me and gripping both of my biceps in her firm grip, "The man is built like a mountain!"

My dad chuckles and nods solemnly. "Aye, that he is."

My sister pats my back and returns to the stove.

I've worked on the farm for as long as I can remember: my parents' plan for me is, at some point, to take over the farm from them when they retire. Although, I can never even imagine a time when my dad will want to retire. At six foot three and built like a tank himself, he's always told us that even amongst the dirt, noise, and stress of the farm, it is the one place where he can find peace.

It is not the place I find peace. It's home for sure, but it is also the place where I spend all of my time hiding the fact that I am gay. The farm is a very macho place, where the men are stereotypical macho men. Talking about girls, breaking open the beers at the end of the shift, a punch on the back, or a slap on the shoulder is the sign of a job well done. Visually I fit right in, my frame wide, muscle on muscle that can only be gained from daily hard graft working the land.

Our moderately-sized farm is equipped with all the latest gadgets and equipment: from tractors, cultivators, cultipackers, and mechanical plows, to the more scientific soil testers and irrigation systems. My dad wants me to learn the basics like he had learned from his father: giving me a quarter acre of land to till by hand and sow seeds on my hands and knees. He says it's character building. What is it? It is the perfect way to get the dirt so ingrained into your skin that it would take a good month of scrubbing to get it all off.

Instead, I left the farm after college and enrolled in the University of Dublin, where I am currently working on my business degree. I'd initially wanted to run a design and consultancy firm once I graduated, which is still a potential option, but the only thing I'm sure of is that I want to build something myself, from the ground up, something that is just mine.

I've stayed in touch with my sister a lot whilst away; she'd guilted me into making sure that I call at least three times a week, telling me that I've left her with a bunch of yokels. I've pointed out those yokels are also called mum and dad, and promised to keep in touch. Dawn found out I was gay a couple of years earlier one night when I'd told my parents I was going down to the barn to muck out the stalls. My sister had been worried as it was a cold night and had brought me a flask of hot coffee, only to walk in on me getting head by one of the farmhands, Jack. She'd promised not to say anything, but it had been too much for Jack, who'd left to work on another farm a few weeks later.

Dawn has kept her promise but has always tried to convince me that I should be open with our parents, that they'll be supportive and loving. I've always made excuses as to why it's not the best time and that I'll tell them when I'm ready. I guess that time is now.

At university, one of the guys in my class had spent most of the first semester eye-fucking me from across the lecture hall. One day I'd worked up the courage to go over and sit next to him. I'd found out his name was Malachi, we'd started dating and have grown close quite quickly. He told me his dream was to move to the States, to cash in on that good ol' New York obsession with Irish Bars, and open his own place. I told him he was nuts but he just kissed me and said I'd come round. I'd scoffed at him, but the thought has taken root in my brain and the more I think about it, the more I can't shake the idea that it's genius.

We'd talked one night after about six months of dating. He'd told me that he doesn't want to date in secret anymore. He'd told me that he'd had bad experiences in the past dating closeted guys, and it isn't for him anymore.

There is nothing left standing between me and telling my parents the truth. I'd called Dawn and told her my plan. She had been excited, and had concocted a plan: she'll cook the family dinner tonight, giving my mother a break, while I come home to help out for lambing season, and tell my parents all about Malachi and me.

"Ok, dinner's ready Pa, wash your hands!" Dawn admonishes him, noticing the smears of dirt still streaked across the backs of Pa's hands. He grumbles but then gets up, quickly washing and drying off his hands before returning to the table. Dawn moves around the table, filling each of our bowls with hot soup, placing large chunks of bread and butter on side plates next to us.

My dad leads us in a short prayer, and we get down to the business of eating. My dad and I wolf down at least two bowls before the rest of them finish their first. It takes a lot of calories to maintain the size of the bodies that we're working with. I feel a sharp kick under the table; my head snaps around to look at my mother, who gives me a sweet smile and continues to eat her soup. A bark of laughter escapes my sister on the other side of me. How she managed to kick me on the other side, I will never know. Dawn gives me a pointed look and tips her head the way of our parents.

I scrunch up my eyes and give my head a small shake, but she reaches out and kicks me again.

"Will you two cut it out?" my mother barks. I roll my eyes at Dawn, who shakes her head and laughs. I see my dad smile at the two of us warmly before standing up to take his bowl to the sink. Dawn's right, our parents are great and they love us so much. It's now or never.

I take in a deep breath and nod at Dawn, whose smile looks like it's about to crack her face in half. I don't want this to be dramatic; I want to get this out the way, field any questions, and then help Pa out down at the barn.

"Listen, Ma," I put my hand on her arm and smile tightly, "Pa, listen I need to tell you something, and I don't want you to make a big deal out of it. I've been seeing someone at Uni, for nearly eight months now, and it's quite serious. He's called Malachi, I'm gay."

There are reactions that you expect to come your way when you announce to your parents that you're gay; shocked gasps, maybe stunned silences, potentially tears. What I don't expect is my father's fist to connect with my cheek so hard, that I hear the crunch of bone underneath as it cracks. I don't expect the blood flowing freely from the jagged open gash on my face to be so warm.

I hear my sister scream as I slip off my chair under the table, banging my head on the table edge and then on the concrete floor underneath. I reach up to grab on to my mother to pull myself up, dazed and unsure of what's happening, only to be stunned when she recoils and pulls away from me.

"Don't touch me!" she screeches. "You're disgusting," she spits before pushing to her feet, moving towards my dad, pushing her face into his chest, and sobbing. I'm not sure what hurts worse, the fire on the side of my face or her reaction.

My sister screams, flying at my dad, her nails out like talons as she claws at his face, gouging out a chunk of his flesh. My mother yells and tries to grab Dawn before she can strike out again, only to be on the receiving end of Dawn's backhanded slap. My mother grabs her face and moves away. The shock is evident in her eyes as she regards us both like we are strangers to her.

Everything else happens so quickly. My parents demand that I leave their house that night and never contact them again. They call me every terrible name I can imagine. My heart breaks as I see my sister beg and plead with our parents to let me stay. When they are unmoved, she begs me to let her come with me. I'm in no place to financially support a fourteen-year-old girl, so with a heavy heart, I have to leave her there. I kiss her on the forehead and tell her she will always be my favorite person. She sobs and wails and tells me that I am hers. I leave the house with a bag of my things, and head to my car and away from home.

CHAPTER 2.

Ten Years Later - 2009

New York City

"Derek, you asshole!" I laugh as the drunk off-duty firefighter spills a third of a glass of Guinness over the surface of my bar. Derek winces and reaches for the bar rag resting on the hook on my side. I swat his hand away and pour him another half, realising that's probably going to be his limit. Derek has been a regular at my bar for the entire seven years we've been open.

Malachi and I finished our time at university, both securing business degrees before spending a year working odd jobs and saving enough capital to finance our move to New York. Securing some investments, we had opened an Irish-themed bar in the East Village of Manhattan. We'd named the bar *The Shannon* after the river in Ireland. We'd told friends it was just because we wanted the bar to have an Irish-sounding name. Still, it was on a ferry tour of the Shannon early one summer evening when Malachi slipped his hand into mine and whispered in my ear that he loved me, before falling to one knee and asking me to marry him. I'd said yes before he'd finished asking the question. Gay marriage was not legal in Ireland at the time, but the promise that he was mine forever was enough for me until we could make it official.

Making a circle of other Irish friends in the City has been a godsend, like bringing a little piece of home to the Big Apple. The bar opening had been a huge success. We'd converted the area at the back of the bar into a small stage space to feature new upcoming folk bands: one of the draws that made us a great place to start a bar-hopping night out. Our place had been featured several times in local media and publications for our diverse outreach, especially amongst the local LGBT community.

We'd lived a very happy life, even though I hadn't thought, after what had happened with my family, that I'd ever be happy again. Malachi had proved me wrong, making me happier than I'd ever thought possible. That was until one evening when he stepped off a sidewalk on the way home from the store and was hit by a city bus. For the second time in my life, my heart was destroyed. They said he was killed instantly and that he wouldn't have felt a thing. It had provided some comfort; I'd been numb. I'd come back to the bar and the deafening silence was too much for me to take. I'd picked up a pool cue that had been propped against the wall and proceeded to destroy every piece of the bar I could reach. It wasn't right that the bar should be here if he wasn't. This bar was his dream.

Collapsing in a heap on the floor, I cried for what felt like hours until one of the bar staff, Lisa, had found me. Fearing we'd been robbed, she ran to me, checking me for injury. I'd told her that Malachi was gone; she'd held me as I cried out my pain, the tears never-ending. She took care of things at the bar, calling in a team of cleaners and tradespeople to help fix the mess I'd made. Closing the bar for a week had been necessary. I'd stood outside the bar the night before we re-opened, the day after burying the love of my life. I couldn't go inside. I'd looked up at the sign, the green neon mocking me with its glow. An idea struck me out of nowhere. I called Lisa, who'd made all the arrangements.

Three days later, I stood outside the same bar, looking up smiling at the new sign above the door. In the same green neon, the name 'Malachi's Place' was now displayed firmly on the front of the building. I felt his presence with me as I walked inside.

That was three years ago.

Now I stand behind the bar, wiping up the spill Derek has made as he glugs back the remainder of the pint in front of him. He tips his glass in my direction, asking for another, a hopeful expression on his face.

"I don't think so, Derek." I reach across the bar taking the glass from his fingertips, then reach further across, snatching the keys from his pocket.

"Hey!" he slurs. "They're mine." He moves to swipe them back from me.

I slide them into my back pocket and he scrunches his nose up at me. "And they will be yours in the morning. Lisa's already texted Christine. She said her shift finishes at the hospital soon, so she'll swing by and pick you up." I nod towards Lisa at the end of the bar. Derek gives her a quick salute before his head droops, and moments later soft snores rumble between his mouth and the wooden bar top. I laugh and grab a clean bar towel from under the counter, folding it up and sliding it under his head.

I turn to roll my eyes at Lisa, but in her place at the end of the bar is Blake Trentnor. Fuck my life.

Blake is the lead singer of Cinder Faith and a constant torment for my eyes and libido. Blake wandered into the bar early last year, and I'd been in no place to notice how extraordinarily hot he was. He'd slipped a CD across the bar one evening when we were slammed with tourists and football fans letting out from the Giants game. He'd asked me if we had any open spots for bands to play since the stage area at the back seemed to have gone unused for a while. It was hard to have that much life in the bar without being reminded of how much Malachi had adored listening to live music whilst we worked in tandem behind the bar.

I'd just been about to tell him to sling his hook when Lisa had dived across the bar, snatching the CD out of his hands and arranged for him to come back the following afternoon with his band to play for the both of us. He'd smiled wide, winked at me, and left the bar. I'd given Lisa a complete 'what the fuck' face, but she waved me off telling me we were losing business on the off-peak to other bars and that she wouldn't let me piss away Malachi's legacy. I'd initially been annoyed for a moment, but she was right. This place deserved to be what Malachi had envisioned.

Blake's band was unbelievable. I'd watched him play, seen the easy way his fingers traveled up and down his Gibson guitar, felt the smokiness of his voice as it caressed my ears. I'd allowed myself to look at him, the thick dark hair and deep soulful eyes, the denim collar open to his chest, the smattering of dark hair there making my stomach clench, the sleeves of his shirt pushed up his elbows, revealing densely muscled forearms. My mouth had gone dry watching him. That had started my year-long obsession with the leader of Cinder Faith.

"Hey, Niall." Ashamed by how my body reacts to the depth of his voice, I nod slightly before turning my attention back to the bar. "How's it going tonight? Busy?"

I turn in confusion to stare at him; he's been here all night as well, he knows how busy we have been. He winces, biting the inside of his cheek and muttering under his breath.

"We've been fine," I grin. I look around to see if Lisa is on the floor collecting empties but I can't see her anywhere. "Have you seen Trouble?" I ask him, indicating the empty spot next to me.

He shakes his head, "No, I think she might have gone to the bathroom. Why? Do you need some help?"

I chuckle and shake my head. "No, it's fine, I think I have it under control here. Plus you just got off stage, you have to be exhausted." His smile is sweet as he laughs lightly.

"I'm good, seriously, scoot over." He comes around the bar, moving behind me to the other side. Between the taps and the fridges, there isn't much room to maneuver around each other. My breath hitches as he presses close behind me; I feel his chest pressed along my back, his breath hot on my neck, his hand gripping my waist as he slides along my body. Fire dances along my skin, where his fingertips grip my hip.

"Hnmphh." I'm not exactly sure what I'm trying to say, but I'm pretty confident I mean it. My cock thickens behind my jeans, moisture starts to form on my chest, sticking the white vest underneath my black shirt to my skin. I crane my neck to see him grin as he picks some empty glasses off the bar and starts loading the washer.

"What was that?" he says, looking at me over his shoulder, mischief in his eyes.

"Oh, it was nothing," I bark quickly, "just clearing my throat."

"Is that right?" he smirks.

I notice that we are 45 minutes until closing time, so I grab hold of the bell-rope and clang the bell across the bar. "Last Orders!" I bellow. "We're closing in thirty." I give myself a fifteen-minute leeway to clear the last of the stragglers out.

"Do you mind if I help you close up?" his voice whispers in my ear as he suddenly appears behind me once again. I bite back a groan and his hand once again finds its way to my hip.

"Lisa is here, she can help me," I finally manage to rasp out.

"Oh, I think I misunderstood your question earlier," he says, mock surprise on his face, "I actually sent Lisa home and told her I was here to help you."

"Is *that* right?" I ask, mimicking his previous question. He bites his lip and goes back to clearing the bar.

CHAPTER 3.

"Goodnight, guys," I call down the street as I close the heavy wooden doors, securing the top and bottom locks, then walking back up the few steps into the bar area. Now the place is empty apart from Blake and me, the space seems thick with tension and claustrophobic somehow.

"Get the last guys out of the bar?" Blake calls, coming in from the small storeroom at the rear of the bar.

"Yeah, they left," I smile. I grab a large grey tray from the bar, moving around the room collecting empty glasses, throwing the empty beer and wine bottles into a large black plastic trash can.

"So we never really get a chance to talk," Blake suddenly shouts, "just you and me, I mean."

I continue collecting the empties and trash, not wanting to meet the stare I know he is giving me. "It would be kinda hard for us to have a good chat mate." I wipe across one of the tables. "Between me running the bar, and you singing on that stage, the only other time you have free is taken up with carting off one of those poor little huge-titted groupies that follow you all around."

A low laugh emanates from behind the bar. "I'm not always picking up groupies," he mock-gasps, "I do have standards, you know."

"Yeah, sure you do mate."

I had spent many an aggravating night behind the bar watching Blake flirting with the never-ending supply of young women who'd come to the bar to moisten the seats whilst watching him and the other boys do their thing. I'd had to ground my teeth on more than one occasion as I watched his fingertips drag from a girl's knee, up her thigh, and rest under the hem of their skirts, whispering things in their ears that made them blush scarlet.

"You make me sound like such a slut." I turn to see him perched on the edge of the bar, legs swinging between the bar stools. A cute pout plays on his mouth. His eyes are alight with amusement.

"Hey, I'm not judging." I hold up my hands in surrender. "You do you." I wink at him.

Turning around, I pick up the large trash can and cart it out to the back of the bar, tossing the contents into the dumpster. I look around the deserted alleyway, the sounds of New York City still loud late into the evening.

I never thought I would get used to living in a place that had no chill. Back in Ireland, once it got to one a.m., the whole world seemed to go to sleep. There were times I would lay awake at night, wishing I was somewhere I could be me. I remember the feeling of isolation, the overwhelming sense of sad loneliness like I was the only person awake in a world full of sleeping.

I look around again at the empty alleyway, inhaling the stale smell of garbage, hearing cars honking, and watching tourists line the street the alley emerges into. I realise amongst the filth and the garbage, that this is truly my home.

I drag the empty trash can back into the building, carrying it behind the bar to store in the back room.

"So is that what you think of me?" Blake asks, his voice lower than before, the humour was gone from his face.

"What?"

"Do you really think I'm just some shallow band member who sleeps with anything in a short skirt? Is that all you think I am?" His eyes have a glimmer of sadness in them. I hate that it is potentially me who put it there.

I walk around the bar to stand in front of him, my hand resting on his bicep giving the hard muscle underneath a light squeeze. "Hey," I prod, "you shouldn't listen to me, what I think doesn't matter."

"Of course it matters!" he growls out through clenched teeth, looking up at me through thick dark eyelashes." I wouldn't have asked you if I didn't care what you think of me."

He reaches up, his hand clasping over mine where it rests on his arm. He squeezes my hand, his eyes locked on mine intently like he is trying to send me some unspoken message. It's just a message I'm not receiving. What the fuck does this guy want from me? He's a straight gorgeous lead singer of a band; I'm just some grumpy-ass gay guy who runs a bar in the middle of the city.

"Niall," he whispers and swallows deeply. I watch as his Adam's apple moves up and down his throat, unable to tear my gaze away. My eyes move unbidden upwards until they lock on to his slightly parted lips. A small choked sound escapes me as I watch his tongue dart out to lick his full bottom lip.

I need to do something before making a fool of myself in front of this guy: all he has to do now is look down to see exactly how much of a fool I'm making out of myself. My cock is leaking like a faucet in my briefs; I just need to get home, tug one out, and shower. I go to move backward away from him but his hand grips mine tighter.

"Where are you going?" His voice is low and dangerous, sending shivers up my spine.

"I was thinking of getting my stuff so we can close up." The smile is plastered on my face, forced, so that I don't do something embarrassing like bite my lip or pant.

"Why?" I go to move again but he holds onto me. "Why do you keep trying to get away from me?" His fingers squeeze mine letting me know I'm not going anywhere. I train my eyes down to my feet, wincing at the noticeable bulge in my trousers. "Baby, look at me."

My head snaps up at his endearment, my breathing quickens as I see his eyes visibly darken. He drops my hand, but only long enough to snag my shirt and pull me to him. His hand snakes into my hair as he pulls me between his open legs. His mouth dips and his lips crash into mine.

I can't stop the needy moan that I gasp into his mouth, my mouth opens long enough for him to slide his tongue alongside mine. The sweet flavour of him is a concoction of the smoky whiskey he drinks and a unique taste that might just become my new favourite. My hands reach up to grasp his shirt, pulling him off the bartop and against me. I rut my hard cock against him, discovering he is just as hard as me. Everything inside me clenches tight as I feel how thick he is, and my first thought is how the fuck am I going to get that monster inside me.

He pulls back and rests his forehead against mine. "Do you have any idea how fucking crazy you make me?" he pants.

"What?" I'm not happy with how many times I've had to ask him what he was talking about tonight. I feel adrift and lost like I'm halfway through a quiz without any of the answers.

"I have to come in here and watch you - watch you talking to other customers, flirting with guys, touching Lisa, all the time wishing it was me you were touching." His voice is strained like he has to force the words out.

"But you're straight," I mumble like a fucking idiot.

He grabs my hand and pulls it down between us. He presses my fingertips along the length of his hard-as-a-rock dick. "Does that seem very straight to you?" He leans forward and captures my mouth in another searingly hot kiss.

Something inside me ignites. I growl and pull his shirt apart, a few of the buttons coming loose, clattering as they land on the floor around us. I pull him to me, trailing open-mouthed kisses over his lips, across his cheek, and down his jaw, enjoying the garbled moans he makes as my tongue draws patterns against his skin. Moving downwards, I bite and suck my way down his neck until I bury my nose into the dark thick hair of his chest. I inhale sharply, smelling the heady mixture of sweat, cologne, and pure man.

I gawp as I discover his left nipple is pierced with a small metal bar. I pull it into my mouth, swirling my tongue around the tightly puckered skin, pulling on the bar with my teeth until he gasps. He grabs the back of my head and pulls me aggressively against him harder, urging me to go deeper.

I look up at him, my lower lip dragging against his chest. "I need to suck your dick," I moan, "please?"

Dropping the cool (or hot) act completely he works quickly to unbutton his jeans, a hint of the young horny guy he once was breaching the calm, confident exterior. I smile as he struggles with the button. My hand closes over his.

"Easy, baby." I try to reassure him. "We have time."

He smiles softly at me; I surge up to meet his mouth. I just can't seem to get enough of him. I reach down, sliding my fingers along the zipper of his jeans, flipping open the button with ease. He gives me a lazy grin and winks.

Once more, kissing my way down his body, I crouch in front of him, pulling his jeans with me as I descend. The first thing that pops into my head as his dick springs forth is *I was not prepared.* What must be ten inches of hot, heavy meat bobs in the air. The fat mushroom head gleams under the lights of the bar, a glistening bead of precum gathering at the tip. I rush forward to collect it with the tip of my tongue. The salty-sweet tang coats my tongue as my body craves more.

"Oh fuck," he growls out above me. Staring up at him I grab his cock by the base giving him a firm squeeze before tapping his hard length against my cheek. I rub the head around my lips, letting the precum saturate the skin. "Please," he grinds out, "I need... I want... god just please."

Never breaking eye contact, I lick a flat stripe on the underside of his shaft, the weight of it making me anxious and excited at the same time. I can't wait to get him inside me. I swirl my tongue over the silky smooth surface around the head of his dick, dipping my tongue into the slit to gather up more precum. God, I'm such a slut for him. There's no way I'm deepthroating him to the base as I have a desire to live and that monster will rip my throat open. Grabbing his shaft by the base, I take as much of him into my mouth as I can, sliding him into my throat.

"God baby, you're so fucking sexy," Blake pants heavily. I reach up and slide my hand along his abdomen, fingertips trailing along the bumpy ridges of his abs, dipping my fingers down the 'v' of his Adonis belt, scratching the skin as I go. "I can't believe we haven't been doing this the whole time."

Picking up my pace as I bob up and down on his dick, my hand undoes my zipper. Pulling myself out, I start to quickly jack myself off, matching the rhythm of my sucking on his cock.

"Baby, please, I'm gonna cum soon, oh fuck I'm gonna…" I suck harder on his dick until I feel the telltale signs of the head engorging and his length stiffening harder still. "Baby, oh fuck!"

Jet after jet of his release hits the back of my throat and coats my tongue. I hadn't thought it possible for someone to cum this much. The intensity of his release gets me there in an instant. I suck on him hard as I spray my release on the floor of the bar at his feet.

Feeling completely wrung out, I slump against him, my cheek resting against his groin. His hands find their way into my hair, stroking me gently. He tugs my face upwards and tips his chin. I move up and he takes my mouth with his. The remnants of his ecstasy on my tongue swirls against his own. He moans lazily into my mouth.

"So why haven't we?" I ask against his lips.

He frowns at me confused. "Why haven't we what?"

I laugh. "Why haven't we been doing this the whole time?"

His hand comes up to stroke the back of my neck. "I just always assumed that you weren't ready," he says cautiously, "you know, after Malachi."

My body freezes like I've been caught with a cold gun. Suddenly the sex haze clears and I realise what I've done. I've sucked another man off in the love of my life's bar. I've degraded myself and dishonoured his memory, for what? A blow job with a hot guy in a bar. So what if Blake gives me the feels in my chest, so what if my body feels alive when he's near? That's no excuse.

Feeling my tension, his hand stills against me. "Baby?"

I tense further. "Oh my god." I grip his shirt tight before pushing myself away from him. "What the fuck have I done?"

"Baby?" he repeats, the worry in his voice clear.

"Please don't call me that, we should never have done this." The disgust oozes out of every pore of me. My heart however clenches tight as I see the pain I'm inflicting on Blake etched on his face. I want to pull him back to me. To push the frown lines from his forehead, because he is so beautiful and I don't want to be the reason they are there.

But disgust wins.

"Listen, I think you should go," I force out. "This was a mistake, we have to forget this ever happened."

"Everything ok?" He tries to reach for me but I step back out of his reach.

"Please, just go," I whisper.

He nods sadly, buttoning himself up. He pauses for a moment. "It's because I said his name, right?" he says suddenly. "You didn't do anything wrong."

"Please," I repeat, unable to continue any longer. Knowing I'll give in if he keeps going.

"I'll go." He steps into my space; lifting my chin with his knuckles he presses a featherlight kiss against my mouth. "Don't let this place become a memorial Niall, you can live here too." With that he gathers his things and leaves the bar, leaving me devastated once more in his wake.

CHAPTER 4.

"Open the fuck up!" The knocking at my apartment door above the bar intensifies. Lisa, by her tone, is clearly annoyed on the other side. I throw my legs off the bed and stumble through the apartment. The six-pack of lager I'd knocked back the night before is strewn across the bedroom floor. I grab my Knicks basketball shorts and slip them on. The last thing I need is Lisa getting an eyeful of my meat and two veg.

"Hold your horses' woman, I'll be right there for Jaysus sake." Kicking my way through the piles of dirty laundry on the bedroom floor, I stumble through the kitchen and pull the apartment door open. "And good morning to you, Sunshine."

She gives me a pointed stare before pushing past me into the apartment, snatching the kettle off the worktop and filling it with water from the faucet. "Right, I'm making us some tea, and then me and you are going to have ourselves a little chat, okay?" She moves to the cabinet, pulling out a red box of Barry's teabags. I love America but they can't make tea for shit. I get tea bags for an extortionate price at an old international food store on Ninth Avenue.

I go back to my room, pulling on an old grey hoodie, stopping by the bathroom to quickly brush my teeth as my mouth feels like someone snuck a sponge into it overnight. Splashing some water on my face and running my fingers through my hair, I go back to face the one-woman firing squad.

Lisa sits at the small bistro-style table in the middle of the kitchen, her arms crossed across her chest, waiting for me to take a seat. She kicks out the chair next to her and nods at it. Rolling my eyes and huffing like a petulant child I plonk down into the seat, picking up the steaming cup of tea she's placed on the table in front of me. I take my first sip and the milky bitter taste I love blasts my senses, waking me up a bit.

"So what's your fucking damage?" Lisa snaps out suddenly.

"Excuse me?" I ask, putting my cup down on the table and turning to face her.

"You heard me." Her eyes widen as if to say *yeah, you fucking know.*

"I don't want to talk about this, Lisa." I turn back to the table, placing my elbows on the surface and resting my forehead onto my fists.

"Well fucking tough!" she barks. "We are going to talk about it because it's been three fucking years Niall."

I grind my teeth together, not wanting to snap at her, but also very aware that she is in my apartment, above my bar, shouting at her boss.

"Listen, I know you miss him, you're going to miss him for the rest of your life. I miss him too." She reaches across and rests her hand on my arm. "But do you think you are honouring him by doing this?"

I turn to look at her, my anger simmering under the surface. "Doing what?" I snap.

"By not living? By just existing in this space? By not letting yourself love again?" She regards me sadly, tears welling in her eyes. "Is that what he wanted for you?"

I don't want to answer because I want the answer to be an absolute yes. I want Malachi to expect me to pine for him for the rest of my life, to never look at another man, and to die just waiting for him to rescue me from this life, just like he'd rescued me from my old life.

But that wouldn't be the Malachi that I loved, that *everyone* loved. He was kind and generous to a fault, he would sacrifice everything if only just to make me smile for a moment.

I shake my head at her, a tear falling free and landing on my arm.

"I had a long conversation with him, you know, about you."

I jerk my head up and wipe my cheek with the back of my hand. "Who, Blake?"

"No, silly boy," she chides, "Malachi. A couple of months before the accident."

I stare at her waiting for her to continue. Malachi was not the type of person to be speaking behind my back without a very valid fucking reason. "What about?"

"About this, actually." She smiles, and my brain is so fucking lost. I don't know whether I'm losing my mind or she is. "Do you remember early in the year when Mal caught that fucker of a flu?"

Remember it? That was one of the worst moments of my life. He had started off just feeling really drained and coughing a lot, until one night when he came downstairs to help me close up. I'd been locking the doors and came back to the bar to find him collapsed on one of the chairs.

He'd been rushed to the hospital. The doctors had told us he had a severe chest infection and would need to stay in hospital to receive fluids and antibiotics because they believed a bacterial infection caused it. I'd been beside myself with panic, but he had convinced me to go home to take a shower, rest, and bring him back some stuff from the apartment. I'd left Lisa there with him, watching over him when I wasn't able to.

"Yeah, it was horrible," I say grimly.

"You'd gone back to the apartment," Lisa starts, rubbing her hands together on the table. "You hadn't been gone five minutes when Mal started getting intense pains in his chest. He was terrified, he thought he was having a heart attack. We called for a doctor, but they assured him it was just the pain from the chest infection and that he would be ok in a couple of days. It scared him, though."

"He never said anything," I whisper, shocked.

"Yeah, he swore me to secrecy," she laughs. "He said that if you caught wind of him having any chest pains, you would likely stop him from cooking a full Irish breakfast every weekend. He said you used to constantly bitch that black pudding is just fat."

I chuckle weakly. "Because it is, pig's blood, fat, and gristle." I shudder.

"Well anyway, when the doctors left I told him not to worry, that he would be fine and that I'd help you guys for as long as you needed me because I love you guys." I put my hand over hers to stop her wringing her fingers. "He said that the scare had got him thinking about you."

"About me?"

"Yeah, like if something ever happened to him, who would look after you."

"Lisa, I don't know if you have seen me recently but I'm a pretty big boy. I don't need anyone to look after me."

She shrugs and continues. "Niall, you were his. He wanted to look after you, and he wanted to make sure that there would be someone to look after you when he was gone. I just volunteered."

My heart somehow constricts and fills at the same time. I was so lucky to have Lisa as my friend.

"Mal made some requests and a wish." She went over to her bag which she had left on the counter and pulled out a sheet of paper. She comes back to the table and hands it to me.

"What's this?" I ask, holding the small square of paper in my open palm.

"It's from Mal, he told me to give it to you when the time was right." She reaches across and squeezes my arm. "I think that's now. I'm going to go start opening up downstairs. You take your time." She gives my arm one last squeeze and leaves the apartment.

My heart is racing, I'm not ready for this. What I hold in my hand is the last time Malachi will ever speak to me. I never thought I'd get to hear him speak to me again, but that's what this is, the last thing Mal will ever say to me. I grab my tea from the table and move to the small window seat, overlooking the street below. Taking a seat, I open the letter.

THE LETTER

Hi honey,

So, hopefully, one day, Lisa will pass this letter back to both of us when we are all old and knocking back tequila shots at our bar, recounting the good old days and swapping stories about our grandkids.

That's what I hope; if you're reading this and I'm not by your side, then it means I've passed. Just know, that is the only reason I would ever leave you. Niall, you are everything to me, and I need you to know that there has not been a single day in all the time we have been together that I've ever regretted.

I want you to know that I am so sorry that I asked you all those years ago to come out to your parents. If I had even an inkling that things might have gone down the way they did… Well, no, I can't say I would have asked you not to tell them because that might have meant we never got to have our life together, and I can never wish for that. They couldn't have known what they were losing when they lost you, because you're the best person I know.

If I'm gone I'm going to need you to do a few things for me:

First thing - If the bar is not the place for you anymore, then just sell. I know you came around to the idea of living in New York because it's what I wanted, but if it's not your passion, then find what that new passion is and don't let anything or anyone stop you.

Secondly - You have to find your sister. I know you're afraid that your parents will have warped her mind and she won't want to see you, but I see you missing her every day. You need her. Promise me.

Thirdly - Give yourself a break. You're always so responsible, looking after me, the bar, Lisa and our friends. Give yourself a chance to be silly and free. I think you might enjoy it.

Fourth - Once a week, eat a massive greasy breakfast. I feel so guilty tucking into my fry-up while you sit there with a banana and yogurt. It's just not natural.

You're going to be back soon with my things so I'll sign off here. I have a wish that I need you to make come true.

Fall in Love.

Please, I need to know you're not alone in the world. I want you to love and be loved. Love with all your heart, the way I love you, and the way I know you love me.

I'll always be a part of you, the same way I know I'll take a piece of you with me.

Be safe, be happy, and please don't forget me.

Your Malachi xxx

CHAPTER 5.

Blake

There are places in New York where you feel most at home. For some people, it's their apartments, the park, a coffee shop, a store. For me, it's the roof of my apartment building. Completely bare, except for the fans and air conditioning units and a single lawn chair that I'd dragged up here a few months ago when I'd moved in.

At dusk, like it is now, the lingering heat from the last rays of sunlight warms my skin and gives me an all-over tingle that I can't explain. The smell from the surrounding buildings' roof gardens infuses the air with a slight perfume without being overwhelming. It's the perfect place for me to write new songs or just play riffs on my guitar.

I'd moved in with a friend from back home in Boston rather than take up the offers of the guys in the band to crash in their spare rooms. Cinder Faith had recently been picked up by a local small-time record label who had promised us big things. They'd had us in a recording studio every weekday morning for weeks writing and recording new material. I loved my little slice of paradise away from the rest of the band.

This evening however, I'm finding it difficult to think of any music to play. It's like the inspiration has been ripped from me, leaving me only with a hollow in my chest that apparently whiskey can't fill. I'd tried. It didn't work.

Ever since I'd walked into Malachi's Place, Niall had caught my attention. His tall frame stacked with hard muscle, the material of his t-shirts so tight they look like they might tear from him like the Hulk. His silky hair falling across his face, getting in his eyes at times, so that he would be forced to blow the strands away so he could see. There'd been nights when I'd sat at the bar and had to dig my fingers into my thighs to stop myself from reaching across and running my hands through that hair.

But there was a sadness in his eyes, an emptiness that I just wanted to help make disappear. I'd watch him flirt with customers, both men and women, in a friendly way. Never with me, though. He would keep himself distant from me. Sure we would shoot the shit, but he would never have that relaxed, easygoing banter that he would have with everyone else, and it made me fucking insane.

I lost my heart to Niall many moons ago, and I had come to accept the fact that he would never be mine. Then last night happened and I finally got a taste of him, a taste of what we could have.

And just like that, it's been all ripped away. That old saying 'better to have loved and lost' is a crock of shit. I still have the taste of Niall in my mouth and I can't see a time when I won't want that again.

I sit down in the lawn chair, my guitar across my chest as I pluck lazily at the strings. The night air is filled with the sounds of the city, soothing me.

"That's not one I've ever heard you play before."

I jump out of the chair like my ass is on fire. Like I've summoned him here, Niall stands just a few feet away. Holy shit. I have to fight the urge to run to him, to tear all those fucking tight well-fitted clothes from him. To finally get a taste of him as he did me.

"What are you doing here? How did you get up here?" I asked in quick succession, not really caring either way, only giving a shit that he is actually here in front of me. That has to be a good sign, right?

"Your roommate let me in and told me where you'd be. I hope that's ok?" He looks so nervous like I might ask him to get out. Kind of like he did to me, but I'd known what the issue was there, and I hadn't been overly surprised.

"Yeah, it's ok, you're welcome here anytime."

He smiles at me and nods his head.

"So yeah, I might have been a bit of a dick to you last night," he says after a quiet minute. I start to say something, but he holds his hands up to let me know he isn't finished. "No, I was, it's been difficult for me, since Malachi died, to get close to anyone. So I haven't. At all."

"What do you mean you haven't…?" I gesture with my hand for him to continue.

"No one since Malachi." He shakes his head.

"But you're always flirting with those guys at the bar," I say, grinding my teeth a bit, hating the thought of him flirting with anyone who isn't me.

He laughs. "Why are you growling?" His eyes are alight with amusement.

"I'm not!" I bite out.

"You are," he chuckles, "You're still doing it."

I hang my head a little, caught in the act. "I don't like it when you flirt with other guys. It pisses me off," I bite out through clenched teeth. I feel a smile fighting its way onto my lips as I see the adorable flush creeping up his neck.

"You don't, huh?"

"No, I fucking don't." I put my guitar down on the lawn chair and move towards him, crowding him against a tall air conditioning unit. "I hate that you would laugh with them, touch them, and not with me." He sucks in a breath. "Never with me."

His hand comes up to rest against my chest. "Do you think it was easy for me? To see you with those girls. You had your mouth on then and all I wanted to do was close the fucking bar so they'd have to leave you alone."

A wave of happiness fills my body. His hands travel up my chest and rub down my arms, gripping me by the forearms. He stops and locks eyes with me, his gaze becoming serious. "I'm not going to say this is going to be easy, but I'm willing to try if you are."

I make an effort not to do a happy dance, instead of biting my lower lip sharply to hold back the smile that threatens to crack my face.

"One other thing Blake," he whispers.

"Mhmm?" I ask, my mouth moving inches forward towards his.

"I don't fucking share," he growls.

"Thank fuck for that." I get out before his mouth slams down against mine.

It's like we both have a hundred hands. I quickly shuck the jacket off his shoulders before lifting the t-shirt over his head. Sex on a roof - classy? Maybe not, but that's what had to happen right now, or I would come out of my skin, and from Niall's reaction, I would guess the same thing would happen to him.

"Get naked!" I bark out. He chuckles quietly, locking eyes with me as he unbuttons his jeans, sliding them down his thighs and kicking them off his feet along with his tan boots. He stands there in only white boxer briefs, and I feel my whole mouth fill with saliva. "Holy fuck," I breathe as I see the impressive bulge pushing against the thin material of his shorts.

"Like what you see, baby?" he says, pushing the heel of his palm against his protruding bulge. I nod, my eyes unblinking, not able to tear my gaze away. He squeezes his cock through his shorts, and I break. I quickly strip out of my remaining clothes, standing naked in front of him. He moves towards me, licking his lips like he is making a beeline for my dick.

"Uh uh," I say, falling to my knees in front of him, "my turn." I shove his hand out of the way and nuzzle my nose into the crease between his thigh and his balls and inhale him in. He smells unbelievable, something I could definitely get addicted to. I run my open mouth along the outlines of his cock through his underwear, wetting the material with my tongue. He pushes his hips forward, looking for friction. Taking mercy on him I pull down his briefs and swallow his cock down my throat.

"Oh my god, oh fuck," he moans, reaching behind himself to grip the hard metal of the air conditioning unit. I hollow out my cheeks, sucking him hard with each thrust of his hips. I move my hands around him, gripping onto two muscle globes. I slide my fingertip down the crease of his butt, and the shiver running through his body vibrates through me. "Ungh." The sound emanates from deep in his throat; he pushes his ass back, trying to force my finger deeper into his crevice.

I pull off his dick for a second. "Don't worry, Niall, I'm getting there. You want me in here?" I ask, tapping my fingertip against his hole.

"Oh fuck yeah, please, I need you inside me." His hand reaches around and rests on top of mine, forcing my finger into his hole alongside his. "Oh god, that's it." The lilt of his accent presses all my buttons. I pull back away from him and turn him round, so his body is pressed up against the cool metal surface.

"What are you doing?" he moans, craning his neck over his shoulder.

"Don't worry, it's just you and me, ok?" I ask, my fingertip still pressed firmly inside his hole.

He nods and then turns back around, his forehead leaning forward.

I massage the globes of his ass with my palms, my fingertip lining the crevice in the middle. Rushing forward, I part his cheeks wide and ram my tongue into his hole. "Oh my god!" A squeal comes from him, higher-pitched than I thought he was capable of with his normal deep baritone. I chuckle for a moment before dipping my tongue back inside him. I stretch him out with my tongue and my fingers until he is panting hard and fucking my fingers with a desperate urgency.

"I need you in me now, Blake!" he shouts. "No more messing about."

Suddenly a realisation hits me like a bucket of cold water. "I don't have any protection with me," I moan.

A deep growl comes from my guy as his fist punches the surface of the metal. He reaches around and grabs my hand. "I haven't been with anyone else for years, and I had my annual physical a few months ago, I'm clean."

I rush to pick up my trousers, fishing out my phone from the pocket and opening up my recent text messages. "I haven't hooked with anyone in about 8 months now, but here is my text from the health clinic from a month ago, all clear."

He grins wide, spits into his palm, and grabs my dick, massaging his saliva along the length, pulling me to him.

"Are you sure?" I ask him, my forehead resting against his back.

He pushes his ass out towards me, the head of my cock pressing against the tight muscle of his entrance. I guess that answers my question. I spit onto my fingertips, lubing his hole up a bit before pushing slowly inside him. I'm more girthy and lengthy than normal, so I know to give him time to get used to me. I continue my slow move forward when he yells in frustration and impales himself on my dick in one swift push backward.

I almost blackout with sensation overload, nothing has ever felt as good as his ass wrapped about me, tugging me deeper from the inside.

"Please, hurry," he gasps, "I'm so close." He reaches down to grab his cock, so I bat his hand away. His orgasms are mine to give. Leaning over him as I thrust into him hard and fast, I make a circle with my fist and let him fuck that as I fuck him.

"I'm not going to last long," I groan into his back as I feel my balls start to tighten up, my climax barreling up my spine at breakneck speed. Before I have a chance to slow down, he pushes back hard and cums into my hand with a scream. This sets my own orgasm off as I pump load after load inside him. I feel wrung out dry, like I might fall over if he is not here to keep me propped up.

After a few minutes, I realise that I'm leaning my entire body weight over his as he slumps against the metal surface. "Oh shit, I'm sorry," I say, kissing his back and preparing to move away.

He reaches and grabs my hand, pulling me so I slide back inside him. Maneuvering us awkwardly to the ground, he lays on his side, pulling my arm around him. "Can we stay like this for a moment?"

I rest my forehead against him, finally sure I am where I'm supposed to be and with who I'm supposed to be with.

"We can stay here like this forever, Niall," I smile, pressing kisses against his warm skin.

"You promise?"

"Forever and ever, baby."

EPILOGUE

Niall

One Year Later

What a year it's been. When he said forever, that fucker meant it. We dated for a while; well, I'm not sure you can call it dating when the guy moves in after two weeks and then you spend every possible moment together either fucking, running the bar, performing on stage, or spending time with our friends.

Blake called the bar to a halt one night. Asked me to come up on stage. He gave a speech on how much I had done for the community, offering food parcels to the homeless, working with local LGBT shelters, offering funding, opening the bar during daytimes for senior classes, and all the other things he had catalogued. He then went into a speech about Malachi, how he had founded the bar, bringing a slice of our Irish home to the States: the hospitality, the warmth, and the welcome. He thanked Malachi for bringing me into his life which just about brought me to my fucking knees.

Then when I looked. He was on his fucking knees. In front of the people at the bar, in front of Cinder Faith, in front of all of our friends, and asking me to marry him. I felt a rush of warmth at my back, I felt Malachi there with me, I felt a move forward. So I said yes, with no hesitation.

Not long after that, things started looking up for Cinder Faith. A local city tour became a state tour, which in turn became a multi-state tour. We hated being away from each other, but we both knew he had to do it for himself and the band. Then came the call for a tour of the UK. He'd be gone for twelve weeks, which was about eleven weeks too long for me. I moped around for a while, until Lisa intervened and said she had hired a new bartender and that she would be assuming the role of manager.

I asked if I had any say in what happened in my bar. She said I totally did, but as the manager, she would overrule me and I could 'get to fuck'. She told me I had to go be with my man and fight off all those groupies that wanted to ride that D. That was all she had to tell me before I was letting his management know to book one extra seat on that flight.

Three weeks into the tour and I'm about ready to let the groupies have that D so I can go back to the hotel and sleep.

"You ok, babe?" Blake presses a kiss against my forehead, stroking the side of my face. "We're here."

"We can't be, we only just left London! Manchester is four hours away!" I yawn sleepily.

"Yeah, that was four and a half hours ago." He laughs lightly, his lips meeting mine. His trick for waking me up is to give me just a taste of him; I always wake up begging for more.

I move my head up, but he moves his back too. "Fucking tease," I pout.

He laughs before pulling me to my feet. "It's just a local bar tonight, no massive stage, so no big set up. Very local, very homey I'm told." Grabbing his wallet and keys from the table on the tour bus, he walks down the steps onto the street.

Manchester, eurgh! It's so cold! It's been a long time since I've been back to the UK. I look out of the window to see the brightly lit bar, glowing neon pink sign hanging outside.

The Desert Rose.

Sounds like a biker bar.

I trot down the steps, wrapped in a huge winter coat, the pedestrians passing the bus in shorts and tight t-shirts since the rule in the UK is 'sun's out, guns out' no matter the temperature. I snuggle up against Blake's back. "As soon as this gig is finished, you are taking me to a swanky hotel and you're gonna fuck me until I pass out, okay?"

He shivers and bends his head, kissing me deeply, sliding his tongue into my mouth. "Thank you for the stage boner," he whines, pushing his hand against his crotch. "We need to go meet the owner of the bar, they said she'd be waiting in the office out back. Come with me and I can ask her if I can set you up there if you don't wanna sit in the crush tonight."

I nod happily, making plans to read a book or catch up with emails while he does his thing.

He pushes the door of the bar open. The other members of the band are setting up their gear along with the roadies and some of the techs. He indicates for me to follow him to the back, asking one of the staff if the manager is in. They gesture to the rooms leading from the back of the bar.

Blake stands in front of a door that is slightly ajar. Giving it a light tap, he pushes it open. "Hey, I'm here to see the… wait." He suddenly stops, "Oh god."

"Hey, I'm Dawn McCullough. You're Blake right, from Cinder Faith?"

A cold sweat breaks on my forehead, I drop my coat and bag to the floor. I'm frozen in time, panic and fear flood my system. I want to move, but I forget how. "Dude, you ok?" my sister asks my fiancé.

"Erm, you might wanna…" Blake says, pointing his thumb over his shoulder at me in the narrow hallway. He steps into the office past her. I catch her frowning at him before she turns her head back to face me.

Her eyes bulge wide, tears immediately springing to her eyes. A harsh sob breaks in her throat. "Niall?" she squeaks incredulously. I somehow manage a nod, unable to do anything else. She stands there for a moment as motionless as me, until her shriek pierces the silence and she throws herself into my arms, her face pressed into my neck as she cries my name over and over. Her agony breaks me out of my trance. I wrap my arms around her, taking us both to the ground. My tears match her own as I kiss the top of her head and try to get her to calm down.

I look past her to my fiancé, the man I love. I know there, and then my life is about to begin again for real.

Yours, Milo

CHAPTER 1.

Milo

"If you need me for anything else, just ask for Milo." I smile at the cute English guy before adding a quick sultry wink, a smile tipping the side of my mouth up. "Anything." I turn and head back towards the bar, putting a bit of swagger in my step. I don't turn around because I know he's staring at my butt, and I want to give him the chance to ogle uninterrupted because I'm charitable like that.

I'd watched the guy arrive earlier in the day with his friend. The friend's potentially the most beautiful girl I've ever seen, with jet black hair, sensual pouty lips, a slender waist, and a nice curve of her arse. If I weren't so taken with the guy, I would have been all over that like white on rice.

"Swing and a miss?" Lana leans across the bar, her larger-than-large boobs resting on the wooden bar top, making some of the male patrons sitting at the bar shift uncomfortably in their seats. That's what happens when you pop a boner over a hot bartender whilst sitting next to your wives and girlfriends.

"Not so much a swing and a miss." I ponder for a moment before glancing over my shoulder at the hot English dude who is still staring over at me. "More of a swing and we'll see what happens."

Lana laughs before moving back across the bar and picking up a bar rag, wiping lackadaisically over its surface. I click my tongue in my cheek before shrugging at her. "I don't think he is ready for all this anyway." I gesture down my body. "He has that lost puppy look."

"Aaaaah," she frowns, "broken heart?"

"Looks like." I nod before taking a seat at the stool facing her.

Lana steals a look behind me before her face pales, and then her expression morphs into something akin to panic. She busies herself at the bar, wiping imaginary dirt from any surface she can find and grinning wildly at the clientele. There is only one reason Lana's face would contort in such a manner so quickly. I swivel around slowly on my seat, like a babysitter about to come face-to-face with the serial killer.

"Nicholas," I state simply.

As with every single time I'm faced with this man, I initially have to fight all my natural instincts which scream at me, *Climb him like a fucking tree now!*. I have to remind myself each time that he is my older brother's best friend. When I say older I mean *Older*. My brother Gio is fifteen years older than me. Our parents affectionately call him their *miracle child* as they thought for a hot minute that they would not be able to conceive after trying for so many years. Finally when they were both in their mid-thirties, they'd had Gio.

I, however, gained the moniker *our little raki hangover*. My mother had mistakenly thought that once you started menopause, you couldn't get pregnant. So she'd stopped using birth control. By the time she'd found out, it was too late. No morning after pill for my mother, no siree.

Finally, I have to remind myself of the most important fact about Nicholas which prohibits me from climbing him like said tree more than anything else - which is that we can't stand each other.

"I'm so shocked," he says blandly. "I'm looking everywhere for you and here you are, sitting at a bar talking to your friend."

"When you say shocked?" I venture.

"I mean you are exactly where I thought you would be, sitting on your arse doing absolutely nothing." He glares at me, which makes the hairs on the back of my neck stand on end. Why does the fact that he intimidates me so much, also turn me on just as much?

"I'm not doing nothing!" I gasp, fake-scandalised. "I was just serving that guy over there." I point over towards the empty beds. "I swear there was a girl and a really hot guy there just a few minutes ago."

Nicholas raises a single eyebrow at me, before looking down at a clipboard in his hands and scribbling some notes. What the fuck is he writing? I bet it's about me. "Sure you were." The corner of his mouth quirks up.

"I was, I mean I would remember. The guy was so fucking hot. I mean like I would have blown him there and then if it wouldn't have gotten me fired." A couple sitting next to me at the bar splutter into their drinks and chuckle quietly. At least someone thinks I'm funny. Patently it's not Nicholas, who narrows his eyes at me, a tic in his jaw and the sound of grinding teeth flashing warning signals to me that I need to shut the fuck up.

If only my mouth is as smart as my instincts.

"Do you think if I run I can catch him?" I point to the stairway up from the beach to the walkway.

"Remind me again why I keep you around, Milo." He heaves a long-suffering sigh, and I almost feel the need to apologise and grow up. Almost.

"Because I'm good at my job?" I smile hopefully.

"Pah!" Lana quickly coughs to cover up her outburst from behind the bar.

"I think if you can't convince your best friend of your worth, then you might be in the wrong line of work Milo," he says sharply before turning on his heel. "Think about it."

I turn and glare at Lana, who smiles sheepishly before escaping into the storeroom. I turn to watch Nicholas walk around the pool. His expression is happy and light as he greets the guests and gives them recommendations of things to do and restaurants around Agios. A knot starts to appear in my stomach, and I shoo it away just as quickly as it forms.

I'm not exactly sure what happened to destroy the friendly relationship I'd once had with Nicholas. He's been my brother's friend for as long as I could remember. My brother had grown up and moved out for university by the time I was three years old.

My mother is English and my dad's Greek. They had met one year when she was on a gap year during university. He had been a waiter at a taverna in town. She'd been travelling alone and had asked him for recommendations on things she must see and do before she left to go back to England. My mother had told me that she had found herself chatting to the waiter for hours. Luckily, his parents owned the taverna so he hadn't gotten fired.

What he did get, though, was a date the following night. They'd fallen in love over the summer. Mum had chosen to abandon the remainder of her travel plans to stay in Agios to spend time getting to know Dad. She told me that she had returned to England to finish her final year at university before returning to Crete. He had proposed the moment she stepped into the terminal of the airport, telling her that he couldn't bear to be apart from her one moment longer. The rest was history.

My parents had moved from the island to the UK so that my mother could look after her own mother who had been diagnosed with dementia. I had only been two years old at the time. So I had grown up a British kid with a Greek dad who missed his home, and a surly older brother who missed his friends. Luckily for him, he'd met Nicholas the first day of university. They were taking the same hospitality management course and were both Greek.

Nicholas had become sort of a surrogate older brother to me, who'd spent the holidays when he could not afford to go home with us. He had never really minded when I wanted to spend my time bothering him and Gio. After my brother graduated, he and Nicholas had moved back to Agios and bought my dad's taverna, and eventually expanded it into a mini-resort.

"You don't think he is going to fire you, do you?" Lana winces, filling up a couple of wine glasses for two older men perched on stools at the end of the bar playing cards.

"No," I shake my head before returning her wince. "I mean, he can't. Gio would kill him."

Lana throws her head back and laughs. "I think we both know that if it came down to it, Gio would choose Nicholas and help hide your body." I can't say the truth of her statement doesn't sting a bit, but she's right. Gio and I aren't close at all.

"I mean he wouldn't," I shrug. "My family's owned this bar for years before he and Gio took it over."

"Sweetie," Lana says, reaching over and resting her hand on my arm. "Gio sold his share of this place fair and square. It's Nicholas's now. He can do what he wants. I think he is just so busy at the moment that firing you is low down on his list of priorities."

"I feel so warm and special inside," I deadpan. "Thank you, best friend."

"Anytime," she smiles, patting my arm before going back to keep herself busy.

I can't even fathom why Nicholas has taken such a dislike to me. I'm so awesome. I get on with everyone; I'm funny, charming, and hot as fuck. I have an arse you can bounce a Euro off and I know that because I kill myself with squats everyday making sure that I can. *Shit, I need to find myself a new job and get out of here.*

"Is this seat taken?" I turn to see a young guy in possibly his very early twenties standing next to me, pointing at the empty stool next to me. I look up at the broad expanse of his bare chest, the patch of dark blond hair between heavy pecs and a washboard stomach that the old widows in the village could scrub their clothes on. I rake my gaze over him shamelessly, my cheeks heating up before I nod at the seat.

"I'm Travis," he smiles, offering me a large hand that could easily double as a baseball glove. I bet those hands could throw me around his hotel room. I take his hand and he squeezes gently.

"Milo." I smile back at him.

"I'm sorry for such a cheesy line, but you must get so bored with men hitting on you telling you how gorgeous you are." He chews on his bottom lip, before looking up at me through his thick eyelashes. "Well I'm sorry but I'm going to be another one." He lifts his hands up and shrugs, like *'what ya gonna do?'*

Maybe today won't be so bad after all.

CHAPTER 2.

Nicholas

Breathe. Count to ten. One, two, three, four and go rip Milo away from that fucking blond giant guy and carry him back to your room and get him naked.

Well, I'm not exactly sure that's how the breathing exercises are supposed to go to keep me calm, but that's what shoots through my head. As I sit in my office overlooking the pool and poolside bar, I watch as Milo laughs at something the shithead sitting in front of him has said and puts a hand on the man's bare chest.

I mean, why not just go ahead and fuck and give the customers something to really watch, since they are just out-and-out fondling each other in public?

He is at work, he shouldn't be flirting anyway, he should be working. I mean, I suppose talking to customers is part of his job. Deep-throating one in the bar area isn't though!

I stand up from my chair and start pacing around my office, stealing glances out of the window on every pass. Anger burns in my chest and my hands fist in anticipation.

So he is just going to flirt at my bar, right in front of me. Then he is going to get that guy's number. They'll go out and Milo will be his usual charming self and before you know it, the giant will have him bent over the end of the bed ploughing into him.

CRASH!

I turn in confusion to see where the sudden noise has come from, only to find my fist halfway through the plywood wall.

Okay, well that's going to hurt in a little while.

"What in the world!" I wince as my office door flies open, and my assistant Helena rushes into the room. A hand flies to her face as she sees my hand disappearing into the wall. "Good heavens, what have you gone and done now?" she gasps. Rushing to grab my wrist, she gently eases my hand out. I wince as I see a fair amount of blood pooling at my knuckles, which now slowly starts to drip onto the tiles below, mixed with the rubble from the broken wall.

"Don't go anywhere," she instructs sharply before going into my bathroom and returning with a damp towel. She pats gently around the wound, cleaning the area before pressing the towel over my hand.

As she takes care of the small matter of my mangled hand, I steal glances out of the window to see Milo still practically fornicating with the arsehole with the muscles. My hand flexes involuntarily again, sending a stinging pain up my arm.

"Oh, now I see," Helena laughs. I snap my head around to see her gaze trained where mine had been, directly on Milo.

"Now you see what?" I bark.

She looks at me, amused, before shaking her head. "You're not as hard to read as you think, Nicholas."

I frown at her as she gestures wildly out the window. "The guy you're in love with is flirting with someone else, therefore you turned into the Hulk and tried to demolish a wall with your bare fists."

I narrow my eyes. "The guy I'm in I…" I stare out of the window at Milo before turning back around and scoffing. "I think you've been reading too much Mills and Boon, Helena."

I turn back around to sneak another glance at Milo when I feel a sharp slap to the back of my head. "Ouch!" I draw my hand up to rub my head when I realise it's my injured hand and yelp, cradling my hand to my chest. "What was that for?"

"What is your problem?" She shakes her head. "It's clear to everyone who really knows you that you are crazy about that boy. What's stopping you?"

"Well, let's just suspend disbelief for a moment and say you're right, that I do love him. Let's count off the obstacles, shall we? His brother is my best friend in the whole world who would kill me if I went near his little brother, surely there is some code about that. Also his parents are kind of like my surrogate parents, which makes him my surrogate brother, and isn't that like incest or something? Also he is so immature and reckless. He is also so young and full of life and I'm an old man now." I look down at my shoes, noticing the dust from the wall and a couple of drops of blood have spattered on their surface. *Great.*

Another slap on the head has me adopting a defensive posture. "What was *that* for?"

"I know you didn't just refer to forty as being old when talking to a sixty-five-year-old woman, Nicholas." I look sheepishly up at her and offer a small apologetic smile. She frowns before moving around my desk and taking a seat in my chair. Helena has been with me for so long that we've transcended the boss/employee relationship and are now firmly in the *she scares the ever-loving shit out of me and I do whatever she says* category.

"You know that boy is crazy about you Nicholas." I snort out a derisive laugh which earns me a glare. "You know I am right. You haven't dated *anyone* since Castor," she says, smirking before slapping some mail down on my desk and sauntering out of the room, shouting over her shoulder, "Go get that hand checked at the clinic."

I had dated Castor on and off for a year before finally ending things officially between us. He had wanted the world when I could barely give him the time of day. The resort had been a handful, and in my head, there was a soft spot for Milo that I just couldn't shake. Castor had asked me to move in with him and I'd turned him down. He'd outright asked me if it had anything to do with Milo. I'd gone off on one about how it would be like kissing my own brother. Even as I was saying it, I could taste the lie resting bitter on my tongue. The final straw had been when Gio had asked me to take Milo on at the resort. I'd no sooner told Castor that Milo would be a permanent fixture when Castor had told me that that meant *he* wouldn't be. We'd broken up that very night.

Helena had been sharp though; there'd been a time many years ago when I would have agreed with her. In his teens, Milo had definitely had a crush on me, which had pissed his brother off to no end. Part of me wonders whether that had been the appeal of the crush for him.

On his eighteenth birthday, Milo's parents had thrown him a birthday party back in the UK. His parents had sent word to his brother that he'd had no choice but to attend. Gio had begged me to go with him, reminding me that I'd owed him since he'd introduced me to Luther, the guy whom I'd been dating at the time. I'd reluctantly agreed, leaving Luther back at the resort to manage things whilst we'd partied it up UK-style. And by that, I mean they'd rented out a community centre, hired a local DJ who sang along and harmonised to the music, and served food such as cocktail sausages on a stick with pineapple and cheese and sausage rolls.

The same as every time we'd gone back, Milo had taken every opportunity to sit as close to me as possible, leaning close to my ear to whisper when he could have easily been heard over the music, stroking my arm absentmindedly. All the times this had happened before I'd laughed it off as some silly teenage crush that he would eventually get over, treating him like the baby brother I'd come to think of him as.

This time had been different though; no matter how much I'd tried to draw on those little brother vibes, they just wouldn't come. I'd spent far too much of the evening noticing how much he had filled out, how his formerly flat chest had disappeared and in its place were two well-rounded pecs. His obscenely tight button-up shirt had showed off every bulge and curve of muscle, and his black skinny jeans had acted as a second skin.

His dirty blond hair had been groomed into a stylish quiff at the front, and to top it off he'd been wearing those fucking glasses. I'd been so used to seeing him in his contact lenses, but that night he'd worn simple wire-framed glasses. My blood had thrummed under my skin, heating me until beads of sweat formed on my temples. Each time he'd touched my arm, fire had followed in its wake.

He'd leaned across me to listen to something his brother had asked him, his chest pressing against mine, his scent invading my senses and overwhelming me until I'd been sure that I was going to short circuit and pass the fuck out.

"Are you okay?" he'd asked me. I'd been too busy making sure I wasn't paying any attention to him, that I'd failed to notice that he had pulled back and was staring at me, our mouths inches from each other. I couldn't stop my eyes from dropping to his full pouty lips, his breath hitching, a soft breath warm against my lips. It had taken every ounce of my willpower to slide away from him out of the booth and rush to the bathroom.

Everything had been different from that point; long gone was the boy who would annoy me and his brother until I convinced Gio to let him sit with us and play games. Long gone was the kid whose playfulness and mischievous nature would make me smile. Long gone was the young man whom I could quite easily brush off as a cute kid who would break hearts someday. In their place was a hot as fuck man who, no matter how much I tried, I could not stop thinking of.

There had been times when Gio's family would come to the resort to visit, and I would need to make myself scarce by hiding in my office or saving off-site appointments for the same date so I would not have to put myself through the torture of being around him and not being able to touch him.

Over time, my bitter arse had turned the desire into frustration, which had led to our current relationship of me barking orders and snapping at him every chance I got.

The first time he'd realised something had shifted between us was the day before he'd come to work at the resort. I'd been happy to try and evade him as much as possible during his infrequent visits and curtail my trips back to the UK. His brother however had begged me to give Milo a shot working at the resort.

What Milo doesn't know is that Gio is one of his biggest supporters. The only problem with that is that Gio is a complete sociopath when it comes to showing the correct emotions. So if Gio wants Milo to toughen up, make new friends or strive to be independent, rather than say 'I'm proud of you, *o aderfòs mou*', he instead opts for '*Get out of my face you annoying little shit, and go get your homework done*'. Stellar brothering!

Milo had been filling in his paperwork with Helena, leaning across the pool bar whilst she told him a story that had him throwing his head back in laughter. I'd stood transfixed at the stretched taut muscles of his neck, the Adam's apple bobbing at his throat, and the lean muscles of his back and arms, because of course he hadn't had a shirt on.

I'd been about to walk over and remind him about appropriate work attire, preferably something in a full ski suit, goggles, and hat so I couldn't see his face or body, when Galen, our bar manager, had sidled up to him, slipping an arm around his waist and pressing a light kiss to his ear.

Closing the distance between us with super quick speed I'd barked, "What the fuck is going on here?" Whipping his head around, Galen had looked like he was about to take a swing at me, until he'd seen who exactly it was. Schooling his features double time, he'd frowned at me, clearly confused.

"What's wrong, *afentiko*?" Grinding his teeth together, Galen had clearly been pissed, but he'd stopped himself from saying anything to risk his job.

"Yeah Nic, what the fuck?" Milo had looked around the pool nervously, a few of the other guests and staff now looking our way due to the scene I'd caused. Deep furrows had appeared in his brow as he gave Galen a quick apologetic glance before dropping his gaze to the floor. It had been shame; I'd made him feel ashamed.

I'd wanted to scream at everyone to get out of my resort so they couldn't see. I'd wanted someone to punch me in the face, if just to stop me from having to experience the guilt squeezing on my chest. I'd like to say that was where I'd stopped, but I'd started and had found it too difficult to back down.

"Milo what the fuck, you have been here five minutes and you're banging the staff already?" I'd said between clenched teeth. What I'd wanted to say was, you've been here five minutes and apparently I'm not good enough for you. It had been childish and ridiculous for sure.

"I wasn't... I mean to say, I haven't been..." he'd started. I hadn't let him finish.

"Milo, I'm not blind, you were all over each other." I might have been exaggerating quite a lot.

"Easy friend." Galen had stepped forward, putting Milo behind him slightly, which had only served to infuriate me further, in that he'd basically been stealing what was mine. "We have been out on two dates, and as far as I'm aware there is no rule that says that co-workers can't fraternise. If there is then I'm sure that you and Elias hooking up in the pool shed a couple of months ago was definitely breaking the rules." Galen had smiled, hoping his attempt at humour had diffused the situation slightly. I'd looked behind him to see Milo wince at his words. *Interesting.*

My righteous anger had run its course. Whilst my blood had still burned the flesh under my skin, Galen's artful dismemberment of my organisational impropriety argument had been vanquished within moments. My teeth had ground together so hard, that I could have sworn I could hear my jaw cracking under the pressure. I'd turned back towards Milo, trying to catch his gaze, whilst he'd seemed to want to look anywhere other than at me, which in itself unlocked a whole new level of torture. I'd screamed silently for him to pin me with one of his stares, for his eyes to cast heated glances down my body, for fuck's sake, to even acknowledge my existence.

"I was just trying to give Milo some friendly advice that it may be best to show some discretion when it comes to *having fun* whilst also here to work," I'd finger-quoted. *Well done dickhead.* I hadn't wanted to wait for the inevitable chatter of gossip to rear its ugly head amongst the staff, who were very clearly watching my breakdown live in vivid colour. Turning on my heel, I'd marched away from Milo and Galen and retreated to my sanctum.

Luckily for my own sanity, Galen and Milo's budding relationship had ended that afternoon. I'd heard on the grapevine that Milo had told Galen that he needed to focus on his job and not rile the boss up any more than he already had. An equal amount of shame and elation had warred within me that day. Shame had finally won out as I'd looked out across the pool where Milo had sat, hanging his head, staring into the azure water. I'd got to witness a tear fall from Milo's face and land in the pool, in turn breaking my heart.

CHAPTER 3.

Milo

My pager vibrates on my belt, rumbling against my groin which is currently pressed up against the bar. This absolute smokeshow of a guy is a total feast for the eyes, and boy am I hungry, the dull vibrations of the pager only adding fuel to the fire of my arousal.

"Do you need to get that?" The deep rumbly voice glides across my ears like velvet. The timbre makes me want to curl up like a kitten and push my head towards him for a good and thorough scratching. "Whoever it is seems quite insistent. That's the third page in a row."

"It is?" My head snaps up to meet the amused gaze of the sexy as sin, tanned god. His mouth quirks up into a hot smirk as he witnesses my brain being frazzled by merely being in his presence.

"Sorry, I think I'm a bit distracted by you." His smile broadens further as I suddenly realise what I've said. "What I mean to say is that you have very nice abs, and I'm distracted by you." *Good play asshole.* "I'm just going to keep my mouth closed now."

"That's a shame." Travis leans across the space between us, his mouth so close to my ear that the heat from his breath skitters down my face, a sweet minty smell invading my nostrils. "It's so difficult to put something in it when it's closed."

A note to you, gentle reader. The correct answer in this situation could be something along the lines of "Why don't we go back to my villa and you can give me a demonstration of what should go in my mouth?" or "I do need something big and hard to suck on, you're right." Instead, I go with:

"Oh it's okay, I've already had lunch." A bark of laughter draws my attention from the other side of the bar. Lana holds a small blue bar towel to her face, her shoulder shaking in silent laughter. She looks up over the blue cloth and rolls her eyes at me. Realisation settles in my gut. I close my eyes tightly and turn back towards possibly the hottest man alive who has just offered to let me suck him off and I'd said no because I had a ploughman's lunch and apparently my stupid brain considers that comparable.

My pager vibrates again against my waist. The small nagging feeling that something is not quite right gnaws at the base of my skull. "Sorry," I wince at Travis, pulling the small black pager from my belt clip. I'd adorned the boring black case with tiny pink stick-on diamonds that one of the guest's children had gifted me. Apparently, she'd been a princess in disguise and I'd been her prince, and to seal our future betrothal, she'd presented me with a small sheet of princess pink heart and diamond stickers.

A cold shiver runs down my spine. Helena's name flashes across the thin LED screen. Now whilst she's a perfectly lovely lady, the fact that I've left three of her previous messages unattended fills me with a sense of dread. Helena is not a woman to be ignored or trifled with. I've seen her reduce strong, burly delivery drivers to whimpering apologising messes with a small sneer and a few well-constructed insults and barely veiled threats.

"I'm sorry, I'm going to have to go." I smile apologetically at Travis, whose face falls slightly, but he nods with a small smile.

"Hey idiot." Lana reaches across the bar and swats me with the bar towel. "Where are you going? I'm sure that can wait." She gestures towards the pager. I turn the screen towards her. Her eyes adjust, and her face drops in horror as she reads Helena's name. "Mate what are you still doing here? Go!" She gestures her arms wildly towards the offices across the pool.

Grabbing my things from the bar top, I stride out of the bar area and make my way across the lush green gardens, the thick prickly grass dense between my toes as I move my arse towards the office.

I reach for the glass doors but they swing inwards, making me stumble across the threshold. My bare feet cool quickly against the blue and white marble floor tiles. I look up to find Helena staring narrowly at me, her arms folded tightly across her chest. My balls immediately retreat for cover as if they sense trouble afoot.

"Hi Helena." I know what tools I have in my arsenal, and one of them is being adorably cute. I know it's crass to blow one's own trumpet, but less face it, if we could do that then we would never leave the house. *Ba dum bump.* I've been told though, that when I smile in a certain way, I can get away with anything. From the looks on Helena's face however, I've been lied to multiple times.

"So you can read then and haven't been murdered." Her eyes narrow further making her brow furrow. "I'd assumed those were the only two reasons I would be ignored by you, Milo."

Duck for cover! "I'm sorry Helena, I was working and didn't see…" I begin, only to be cut off by a severe tutting.

"Oh don't bullshit a bullshitter dear." She wags a manicured nail in my face. "If by work you mean propping up the bar with the hot gentleman in Room Six?"

Abort! Abort! Roll over and show her your belly! "Sorry?"
Rolling her eyes, she turns on her heels and walks towards
her office, beckoning me to follow her.

"There has been a bit of a situation that we need a hand
with." Her voice now takes on a quieter tone as she opens
the double doors into the managerial offices. The melodic
hum of the fans overhead as well as the sweet perfume
permeating the air from the Jo Malone diffuser on Helena's
desk makes a heady concoction that gives the entire place
a Turkish spa vibe.

"We?" The cool pit of dread from earlier comes back with a
vengeance. She hasn't mentioned the name yet, but I feel
it coming. Like when you can sense the arrival of a storm
moments before it happens.

"Yes there has been a small problem where Nicholas is
concerned," Helena whispers.

"Oh hell no!" I hear the deep voice booming from the other
side of the door leading into the boss man's office.

Helena squeezes her eyes closed and gives her head a
small shake. "I was maybe hoping that he wouldn't hear
that," she winces. The wooden door slams open, hitting the
metal bookshelf that stands against the wall, making a
harsh clanging sound that echoes down the corridor.

I might be a glutton for punishment. Framed in the dark
wood doorway stands Nicholas, all six foot three of him.
His muscle-bound chest bulges under his shirt like the
freaking Hulk, trying to tear its way through the fabric. His
dark hair is long but tied up into a loose bun on top of his
head, two stray tendrils falling over his light blue eyes. The
dark hair contrasts his sun kissed skin amazingly. The
anger in his face only serves to give him a brutally sexy
scowl that makes my balls clench and my dick bob in my
shorts.

"Call someone else," he bites through his teeth, "I don't want it to be him."

What an arsehole! "Hello to you too," I shrug. "Rude."

"See!" He gestures towards me quickly, before wincing and pulling back a clearly injured hand to his chest like a wounded dog. A white bandage is wrapped loosely around it, but small red spots give away some of the obvious trauma underneath. My heart catches in my throat.

"What the hell happened?" I gasp, rushing towards him instinctively, my hand reaching out to grab his wrist, pulling his hand towards me. I stroke a finger down the side of his hand. The blood underneath the bandage starts to stain the cloth more prominently. A slight hiss from his mouth is followed quickly by a hitch in his breath. I chance a glance upwards to see an undeniable heat in his stare. I gulp deep in my throat.

He pulls his hand away from me quickly and turns his back, retreating into his office. "Find someone else."

"Not happening!" Helena calls back through to him.

"What happened?" I ask her.

"You know how he is," Helena smiles, her eyes darting around the room. "He gets a bee in his bonnet about something or other, and the next thing you know... tada!" she sings, pointing towards the door to his open office. She gestures for me to follow her.

Nicholas stands facing the window, the sunlight casting his shadow across the room. If he weren't the world's biggest arsehole I would have no problem crawling across the cool tile floor on my hands and knees, begging him to touch me for just a moment. Pity is, he's my brother's best friend and indeed holds the title of world's biggest arsehole. Actually maybe he's tied with my brother for that title.

"You likely have a break in that hand Nicholas," Helena barks next to me. "There is no one else free to take you. You cannot drive yourself, and Milo here is free to drive you to the A&E department."

"Milo is what now?" My head spins towards her. "Oh, I don't think I'm the right person to be left with that kind of responsibility. Ask Lana or Jules. Or even better, ask Frank from maintenance. He hasn't had a chance to use that golf buggy for a while. He'd jump at the opportunity."

Helena rubs her temples and sighs. "Not you as well! I can only handle one temperamental dickhead at a time. Lana is busy tending bar. Jules is off today and Frank can barely see, which is why we hide the golf buggy in the back sheds where he can't find it."

"Helena," Nicholas starts as I begin to make my own objections and further suggestions.

"No buts!" Helena snaps. "It is settled. Nicholas, you need to go to the hospital. Milo, you are obviously not busy. Accept your fates, the pair of you. Now deal with it like adults." With that she marches out of the room, slamming the door on the way out.

"So..." I whistle. "How did you do that?"

"It's nothing. I let my temper get the better of me," he mumbles, sliding down into his seat.

"What made you so angry you decided to Hulk-smash a wall?" My mouth gapes as I notice the giant hole in the wall to my right.

"I was watching when..." He seems to catch himself before shaking his head and smiling. "Wasp."

"Wasp?" I frown.

"Yeah, I hate the sting-y little bastards," he shrugs.

"No shit." I eye the wall once more. "Listen, I know you don't like me, but from the look of that bandage, we really need to get you fixed up. Shall we just go before Helena has to come back in and shout at us some more?"

He chews on his bottom lip, his eyes trained to the desk in front of him. "I can make my own way there." He reaches for his phone, again realising a moment too late that his dominant hand is pretty messed up. "Maybe I can't," he breathes heavily.

Am I really that bad that I can't be trusted in an emergency to drive someone to get help? I know my family consider me a screw-up and my friends think that I am chaotic in a funny way, but surely I can be trusted to do this small thing! "I'm sorry you're left with me," I say, trying to paste on a smile but likely ending up showing him a sad grimace. "I wish there was someone better to take you. I promise I'll be quiet and you won't have to deal with me at all."

"I trust you," he mumbles, somehow reading my thoughts. He pushes himself out of his seat, grabbing his wallet and phone and pocketing them. "I sometimes struggle to trust myself, is all."

CHAPTER 4.

Nicholas

Okay, why the fuck would you say that? is the prevailing thought that taps against the periphery of my brain as I try to ignore what I hope is a very near miss of what would have been a shitshow.

Milo drives us fast, or as fast as his little red boxy car can go, being a 2008 Suzuki Celerio, down the A90 towards the main district hospital in the centre of the town. I stare out of the window at the passing dry brush that lines the side of the motorway and the small villas built on the side of the hills that are scattered around the Cretan countryside, and the Kandylakia roadside shrines that just appear out of nowhere all over Greece every now and again. Basically anything to keep my eyes busy and stop me from meeting the gaze of Milo, whom I am sure has been stealing glances at me every few seconds.

"I can feel your eyes on me," I bite out through my teeth. "Everything okay over there?"

Milo clears his throat and gives his head a small shake. "No, nothing." It definitely isn't nothing.

I let it go as we continue to weave in and out of the traffic. The town slowly starts to build up around us, until there are hotels and trinket shops and tourist traps as far as the eye can see. The hospital comes into view as the car slows to a gentle stop at the curbside. Opening his door, Milo quickly runs around the car. I watch curiously as he opens my door like a gentleman letting his lady friend out after dropping her off home. "You know I have a perfectly good hand right?" I smile, wiggling the fingers of my non-mangled hand.

"I've heard plenty of men say that and I've always proved them wrong." Milo gives me a lascivious wink, chuckling low in his throat as he reaches across me to undo my seatbelt. I push my hips back into the seat in hopes that he won't cast his gaze across my sudden and severe boner pushing urgently against the inside of my zipper.

"Ahem, Milo…" I cough, hoping to diffuse the situation enough that I don't push forward and slam my mouth up against his.

He pulls back until his mouth is mere inches away from my own, his sweet breath blowing gently across my lips. "Go and get yourself checked in. I'm just going to park the car and I'll be right with you." He steps back away from the car and helps me to get out, securing my arm as I use the door handle to yank myself out onto the pavement.

Milo pulls down the road toward a large multi-storey car park as I make my way inside. This is getting out of hand. I've established our relationship into a format in which it totally has to remain. I'm the grumpy boss who snarks and snaps, and he's the flighty sexy young employee and little brother of my best friend whom I absolutely can't have naked in my bed. Although that's what my body is screaming at me to do at least once a day.

The triage nurse at the desk gives my hand a once-over, takes some details and points at some gaudy burnt orange plastic chairs that line the edges of the corridor. I assume that means she wants me to sit there and not witness just how god-awful they are.

I slide down into the chair, my butt immediately protesting as the plastic tries to force the muscles in my arsecheek to mould to its oddly-shaped curves. *Stupid squats*, said no gay man ever.

"So what did they say?" Milo takes the seat next to mine and slaps my thigh quickly. The hand imprint from the swift slap causes my skin to tingle, but inexplicably the tingle radiates out through the rest of my body at the contact. *Keep it together, or Gio will murder you in your sleep!*

"Just waiting. You don't have to stay; you can go back to the resort and I'll get someone to pick me up later. I might be here a while."

"Then you won't mind some company then," Milo says simply, pulling a book out of his back pocket, stretching his taut legs out in front of him and settling back.

A few minutes pass with no conversation. People pass us by without paying much attention, trolleys with patients are wheeled from room to room, families and relatives arrive with flowers and bottles of an energy drink as is the custom for a hospital stay. There's something about stepping into a hospital that makes people immediately assume you need flowers from the garden and an energy drink, like you're about to attend a rave at the Chelsea Flower Show.

"So why did you really punch the wall Nicholas?" His voice startles me. I push myself up, my back straightening in the chair.

"I already…"

"Please don't start with that wasp nonsense." He peers at me from under his eyelashes. "We both know that's not true."

God, how does he know? He can't know. He must think it's something else. What on earth would he think made me so angry I put my own fist through my own wall? I haven't said anything and he is just staring at me. His mouth is so plump. Those lips were made for kissing. No those lips were made for ME to kiss them. I don't want anyone else but me kissing those lips. If I hadn't had punched the wall he would probably be using those lips on that stupid guest at the bar. He might be on his knees with his lips around his…

"There!" Milo jabs a fingertip into my bicep. "What on earth are you thinking of that's making you so mad? You're clenching your injured fist and grinding your teeth."

"It's nothing." I shift in my seat, looking down the corridor desperately, praying for a doctor to come along to speak with me to get me out of this awkward spot.

"What is with you today? You're so cagey," Milo whispers. "Is something going on? Have I done something to upset you?"

"You mean more than you normally do?" I try for a smile, but from the look on his face, he isn't buying what I'm selling. "I told you, it's nothing."

Milo huffs and goes back to reading his book, his fingers curling around the pages as if he's trying his hardest not to rip the pages apart in sheer frustration. I don't like that his frustration stems from me, but this is the way it has to be. We don't always get what we want in this life, no matter how great I think we could be together. Sometimes we have to make sacrifices, and this is mine.

"Listen, it's not going to matter much soon anyway. You can go back to your chilled-out existence," Milo sighs, rolling the book into one hand.

My head turns sharply towards him. "What is that supposed to mean?"

"It means that it was a mistake for me to come and work with you. You own the place now, so I think I'm going to find somewhere else to work and if that fails I think…"

My stomach churns as panic starts to tingle along my arms. "What?" The word comes out of my throat like a mouse's squeak.

"I think I'm probably going to move back to the UK. Really give you that space you need." Milo smiles sadly, placing his hand on my knee, using it for purchase as he pushes himself to his feet. I knew intellectually he doesn't mean right at this moment, but there is some kind of finality in his moving away from me right now that my brain just cannot handle. It likely explains why my hand shoots out at that moment and grabs hold of his wrist tightly, pulling him back sharply towards me until his face is so close to my own I can see the flecks of green in his eyes.

"You can't just leave me," I whisper, the mere thought of him getting on a plane and not coming back catching in my throat and making it feel like I'm trying to breathe underwater. My hand tightens a fraction further on his wrist, as I fight the urge to pull him the rest of the way forward and get a taste of him at long last.

"Nick?" A sharp cough to my left breaks the spell between us. Milo jumps back quickly, his fingers pulling at the hem of his t-shirt to straighten it. I somehow drag my eyes away from Milo to aim a glare at the person who for all intents and purposes is the cock block of the century. I am not prepared.

"Castor?" My mouth hangs open. Standing in front of me, looking between myself and Milo with a very pronounced frown on his face is my ex-boyfriend. Castor is a doctor at the hospital so I'd known there was a chance that I would run into him, but not with Milo all up in my face.

Castor looks disapprovingly between me and Milo, frowning before shaking his head sadly. "So Nick, looks like you have been through the wars."

"He punched a wall." Milo's voice is suddenly loud and echoey in the small corridor. "Sorry," he winces.

"You're Gio's baby brother right?" Castor smirks, looking mutely at an open light brown file in his hands.

"I don't know if I qualify as a baby." Milo bites the inside of his cheek. "But yeah, that's me."

"It was nice of you to bring your boss to the hospital," Castor shoots back. "Most employees would likely be eager to get back to work and relax since the boss is incapacitated." If Castor thinks he's being subtle by hammering home Milo's status as my friend's brother and the fact that he is my employee, he is mistaken.

"Castor," I sigh.

"Sorry." He turns to me and smiles. The warm genuine smile that I'd woke up to most mornings, the same smile that had won me over on our first date, walking along the seafront on Almyros beach.

"You're Nicholas's ex-boyfriend right?" A tight smile appears on his face, but one that does not reach his eyes. "I remember you from when I used to visit."

"That's me." Castor winks at Milo before turning his full attention to me. "Nick, what have you gone and done to yourself?" His hand lands on my shoulder, running slowly down my arm to give my bicep a squeeze. "Let's take you to X-ray to get you checked out. I'll take care of you."

I don't want him to take care of me, I want to just go back to moments ago with Milo. It's insane and I know I'll pay for it later, but I know without a shadow of a doubt that I'm going to tell him everything. How I feel, why I have treated him the way I have, and just why I'd punched a hole in a wall. Right then however, said hand begins to throb. I need to get this fixed and some strong painkillers down me so I can talk to Milo without the bleeding wound in my hand.

"Okay let's go." I smile at Castor. "Are you okay here?" I turn to look at Milo.

"Yeah, I'll be fine. Go with Castor." Milo smiles at me for a moment, a war playing out on his face until something in him breaks. Moving quickly towards me, he throws his arms around my shoulders and squeezes me to him. I feel his heart beating rapidly against his chest, matching pace with my own. *Fuck the painkillers*, I want to shout at Castor, *just get me a sling or a cast so I can take this man home*. Milo pulls back and kisses me gently on the cheek.

"Let's go." Castor nods down the corridor towards what I assume is the X-ray suite.

"I have to go." My hand runs down Milo's bicep, down his forearm to squeeze his hand. "Thank you for bringing me here though."

"We should go, Nick," Castor speaks. "The technicians are waiting."

"It's fine, go." Milo chews his lower lip. I nod and follow Castor down the hall until he suddenly stops.

"Shit, I forgot the chart at the nurses' station, wait here for me." Castor runs down the corridor to collect his things before appearing a couple of minutes later, light brown file in hand. We walk side by side into the X-ray suite's waiting room, Castor books me in and sits with me while I wait.

"I can't believe you're here Nick." Castor nudges my shoulder with his. "I've thought about you a lot."

"Really," I laugh. "From what I hear you took our breakup remarkably well and have made a point of hooking up with half of Malia."

"That's not fair Nick," Castor sighs. "I was hurt when we broke up and yeah, maybe I rebounded a few times, but can you blame me?"

"It's all in the past now anyways," I shrug. "No need to explain anything to me."

"What if it doesn't have to be though?" Castor murmurs.

"What do you mean?" I turn to catch his eye, but his gaze is fixed at the file on his knees.

"We were good together Nick." A small smile plays at the corners of his mouth. "I've really missed you and I've never really gotten over you."

"Castor…"

"No, listen Nick." He turns to meet my stare. "I've been thinking about us a lot and I know that I was unreasonable and that I shouldn't have made you choose, but I was feeling insecure. But I love you, Nick."

"Castor, I'm sorry but no." I have to be completely clear.

"No?" His brow furrows.

"I mean, you were right, you deserve someone who will put you first, who won't think twice when you want to move things along in the relationship. I only came to realise after we broke up that I was not the right person for you. I loved you Castor, but not in the way that I should have, not in the way I…" I stop in my tracks.

"Not in the way that you do Milo," Castor finishes for me. My silence answers a thousand questions.

"I'm really sorry."

Castor waves me off, standing from his seat to check with the technician how much longer we'll be waiting. Every second feels like an hour, and every hour a year as I count the milliseconds until I can get back to Milo to tell him exactly how I feel about him.

It doesn't matter how long I wait, because by the time that I get out of X-ray, Milo is already gone.

Chapter 5.

Milo

"Hey Milo!" I turn to see Castor jogging back down the corridor towards me.

"Hey Castor, what's up? Did you forget something?" I ask, looking back to where we'd been sitting.

"No, I just wanted to ask." Castor bit his bottom lip. "Is Nick seeing anyone?"

I want to scream, *Me! He's mine!*, but that was all just in my head as evidenced by the gentle brush-off I'd just received. *Thank you for bringing me?* What the fuck was that? That's what you say to the taxi driver who brings you home after a drunken night out, not the person whom it'd seemed you were just about to kiss.

"Erm, I don't really know. No, I don't think so," I shrug, aiming for nonchalance.

"Good! I'm going to see if he wants to try *us* again. He seemed really surprised but happy to see me. I can still feel the connection." My stomach sinks to the floor. "Well, I'd best get back to him. Hopefully, I'll be seeing you around a lot more if it all works out." Grabbing a paper file from the nurses' station next to him, Castor gives me a small salute and jogs back down the corridor.

I step back, sinking down into the ugly plastic chair. My head drops as a sad chuckle escapes from between my lips. Of course Nicholas would want to be with someone like Castor: he's handsome, patient, successful, and likely doesn't give Nicholas deep furrows on his brow like the ones that appear during bouts of sheer frustration that seem to occur whenever I'm around.

With one final deep sigh, I push myself to my feet and walk to the nurses' station. The slightly harangued-looking woman peers up at me from heavy eyelids. "Can I help you, young man?"

"I'd like to leave a message for the guy who just left with that doctor, Nicholas."

"You can go back there, you know." She points towards the double doors down the corridor. "He might be here for a while, three or four hours at least by the time the radiologist gets a look at the X-rays. I can go see if it's okay with him if I send you back there?"

"No, don't disturb him, but if he asks, can you please tell him that I am sorry and that something came up?" I turn on my heel before she has a chance to say anything else. During the whole walk to the car I keep mentally kicking myself. I've been sure that, at some point today, I've felt something between us. Of course there isn't though; if there had been anything between us, he would have said something after weeks and weeks of me parading different men around the resort and around town every chance I got, rather than looking at me like an annoying little brother that he just can't shake.

Could I have been reading everything wrong though, all this time? Could the irritation really be frustration driven by the green-eyed monster? A small thrill of hope grips my stomach at the thought. A hope that I quickly extinguish. He's back there right now getting back with Castor and quicker than you can say *anal sex*, Castor will be back with Nicholas and I'll need to watch them fawning all over each other.

Can I do that? In all the time I've been working back at the resort, Nicholas has never had a man around. He's always been the incredibly sexy, boner-inducing, wet dream-causing grumpy boss man who won't give me the time of day, let alone his dick. Now I'm expected to just sit idly by whilst I watch somebody else lap up what I want. I might not be able to stop it, but I sure as hell can make sure I'm not around to witness it.

Half an hour later I have my backpack loaded into the back of my little car and Lana is standing awkwardly near the driver's side door. "Come here silly," I laugh, pulling her to me for a hug.

"I don't understand why you are just leaving," she pouts. Her luscious bottom lip sticks out in a very cute way. I'm sure If I were a straight guy it would have at least some effect on me. "It's all a bit sudden and out of nowhere."

I'd called Helena on the way back to the complex and told her I would need to take some extended time off with immediate effect. To say she wasn't pleased would be putting it mildly, but cryptically she'd said that she was surprised I was going anywhere at all given the circumstances, and she'd refused to be pushed to explain when prompted.

"I just need a bit of a break, you know, from this place. It seems like everything important in my life has been attached to this place. Maybe it's time I try and find something new to be important." I give her one last squeeze before pulling out a white envelope from my shorts pocket. "Can I ask you to give this to Nicholas when you see him next?"

"Is this like your resignation or something?" She holds the envelope gingerly between her fingertips as if it's some type of dangerous explosive that might go off at any moment.

"You could say that." I pull her in for one final squeeze. "Listen, I'm going to have to go. I managed to score a flight on Dimitra's dad's jet, but it's wheels up in an hour and a half so I have to leave."

"It's not gonna be the same without you here Milo." She presses her face into my chest, sniffling for a moment before giving herself a little shake. "Go on now, don't miss your flight." She shoos me away.

An hour later I pull my small car into the private hangar at Sitia Airport. Dimitria stands at the foot of the steps of her father's Learjet 60. Her name is brazenly emboldened on the side, a true daddy's princess. "Hey Babe!" she squeals, running the short distance to me and grabbing both of my hands, pulling me physically up the steps of the plane. "We are going to have such a great time in London."

It was one of the things I love about Dimitria, she would never let a little depression or heartbreak get in the way of her having a good time.

"Yeah I hope so hun," I sigh, "I need a bit of mindless fun."

"I don't know if I can help you there," she frowns, clearly troubled, "but maybe you can see if one of Daddy's air stewards is into that. Maybe you could go into one of the bathrooms?" Her face brightens immediately as she scans the hanger for appropriate men.

"Jesus Dimi!" I laugh. "I mean like a night out in Soho, not a quickie in your dad's jet."

"Oh now that I can handle!" she smiles.

The jet roars down the runway, the wheels lifting off. The familiar pressure downwards as if I'm being physically pulled back towards Crete. *I'm making the correct decision, right? This is the grown-up thing to do. Move on. Grow up.* Maybe I do just need some mindless fun. What's the old saying, *best way to get over a man is to get under another one*. So why the hell do I feel so heartbroken, and why am I so sure that no matter how much I try now, I won't be able to move on?

CHAPTER 6.

Nicholas

A white temporary cast adorns my wrist. A break to the scaphoid bone in my hand is going to have my hand out of commission for the next six weeks, which sucks because it means that I'll either need to rely a lot more on Helena, which I don't like to do, or hire a temporary manager. Most likely I'll ask Lana to step into my shoes and get some temp bar cover. It would make things easier, and Lana knows exactly what she's doing when it comes to running the day-to-day of the resort. It isn't that I can't work with a cast on my hand, but the majority of my day-to-day involves fixing broken things that don't really need the expertise of an expensive handyperson and making sure the books are balanced so the accountant keeps off our cases.

Lana's a dab hand at fixing things. I've seen her under the bar with a wrench and pliers fixing the beer lines and re-wiring faulty light cables whilst simultaneously tending the bar. She's the obvious choice.

The nurse filling a clear plastic bag with a couple of boxes of painkillers and anti-inflammatories is droning monotonously on about the hygiene and cleaning routines I'll need to follow whilst wearing this clunky thing on my hand. In all honesty I just want to get the hell out of here as quickly as possible. It's been four hours of the longest, most awkward doctor/patient interaction I've ever had the displeasure of being part of.

After I'd made it clear to Castor that I had no interest in starting things back up with him again, he had immediately withdrawn and stayed quiet for the majority of my stay. He had left when the radiologist had taken over, and I'd been stuck in a bland cream-walled clinic room waiting for the rest of the time.

The only thing I'd actually wanted to do was to get back out to Milo. I'd had plenty of time to think and I couldn't think of one reason to not tell Milo how I really felt. I mean, yes, might his brother and my best friend break my jaw? Absolutely, but jaws heal. Is it maybe not really appropriate to date an employee? Without a doubt, but I could just fire him and then bring him to live with me and he could find another job. Is there a huge age difference and does that age difference usually lead to him annoying the living daylights out of me? Oh yes, without question.

Do I love him? Also yes, without question.

I push my way through the doors into the reception area and scan the seats along the back wall. No sign of Milo. Cranky Nurse is still sitting in the same spot, looking as if she hates life and everyone who dares enter the doors of the hospital. She rolls her eyes as I approach.

"Yes sir?" she sighs.

"The bo… the young man I came here with, do you know where he went?" I give the corridor another quick scan to make sure he hasn't returned whilst my back has been turned.

"Oh yes, the young gentleman." She taps her pen on the desk in front of her. "He told me to say that he was sorry and that something else came up. Did you want me to call you a cab, sir?"

What the hell could have happened to make him leave in such a hurry? I would assume, if some kind of disaster has befallen the resort, Helena might have thought to include me in the list of people who might need to be informed. I'd stupidly left my phone on my desk when I'd followed Milo out to his car. I'd been far too enthralled by how his ass was perfectly cupped by his shorts to remember to pick up important things like my phone.

Half an hour later, the silver Mercedes cab pulls up at the gates of the resort. Chucking the guy enough Euros to cover the trip as well as a nice tip, I wave him off back towards the main road. Walking swiftly through the resort past the guest houses and the main complex, I head straight for the pool bar. Sure enough, Lana leans across the bar smiling at an older couple. She passes them across what appears to be two large pina coladas with all the bells and whistles coming out of the top of them.

Her eyes dart to me as I approach, a deep frown appearing on her brow. "Lana, is Milo somewhere around here? He kind of ditched me at the hospital."

Lana turns to the couple sitting at the bar and murmurs an apology before nodding her head off to the side. Slinking down the bar, I slide onto one of the tall bar stools. Lana reaches under the bar top and pulls out a letter. She regards it with an air of sadness before sliding it across the countertop towards me. I stare down at the envelope with caution, somehow knowing that I am not going to like what's inside.

"What's going on?" I look from the envelope to Lana.

"I think you should probably just read it." She hooks her thumb over her shoulder. "I should get back to the guests."

Where the hell is he? I cast a quick glance across to Lana, who appears to be regarding me with a level of caution that is nowhere near normal for her. My eyes drift back to the letter which is pressed to the bar by my fingertips. Like ripping off a plaster, I pick up the envelope and tear it open, pulling out the piece of lined A4 paper folded up neatly within.

I reach across the bar and grab an unopened bottle of water from the shelf behind it, popping the lid open and taking a giant swig. I may or may not be stalling for time. The way Lana handed it to me makes me think that this is a letter I should hold off reading for as long as possible.

If Milo were here, he could read this for me.

With a deep sigh, I unfold the paper.

Nicholas

Ok so I am going to warn you in advance that the contents of this letter are not meant to make you feel awkward or uncomfortable in any way. It was my hope that what I am about to tell you would have been welcomed and maybe even eagerly reciprocated, but after today I am assured that it won't be.

First and foremost, I want to say thank you for giving me the opportunity to come back to spend some time at the resort. It meant a lot to my family and I am happy that in a way it will be kept within the family.

So here goes. When Gio brought you home for the first time, it was like something clicked inside of me. I didn't know what it was, like some answer to a riddle that was on the tip of my tongue, but it just wouldn't... you know.

I knew that I wanted to be around you all the time. I loved watching you chat with my parents, the way your jaw would click and tense whenever my dad would say something not very politically correct, but you were

too polite to say anything and you just wanted them to like you.

Every day you spent with my family; it was like you were unconsciously teaching me things about myself. Like how when I was nine years old, we were at that beach down Southend-on-Sea, remember? You and Gio were visiting us and had taken me, the annoying little brother, to the beach. Gio was telling me about how I would meet a girlfriend someday and I would leave you both alone. Then you took off your shirt and went jogging down the beach. I think it was that moment that I knew that I would not be bringing a girl home any time soon.

At my eighteenth birthday party, I really thought that you were going to kiss me. My heart was pounding so fast. I'd had really strong feelings for you up until that point. I remember looking into your eyes and seeing the affection there reflected back at me. I think I fell completely and utterly in love with you at that moment.

I hoped that it would go away over time but it never did. I watched you from afar, but up close. I watched you when I was back in the UK and you were getting serious with Castor. It broke my heart, but Gio had told my parents how happy you were, and I knew in that moment that your happiness meant more than my broken heart.

When I came here to work with you I prayed that it was just a childhood crush, that the fantasy wasn't what I'd built up in my head. It wasn't the case though, I wanted you so badly each and every day. But it seemed that the more I wanted you, the more you came to despise me. I don't know what I did to piss you off so much, but I need you to know that I never meant to. I used to give you a hard time because it was the only way I could think of to be close to you.

Today I thought there was another moment between us. I thought that maybe I wasn't so crazy and it wasn't as one-sided as I thought. I think I was going to tell you today how fucking much I loved you. Then Castor told me how you two were getting back together and I just couldn't bear it.

I know this probably makes me childish, but I can't just sit there right now and watch you play house with someone who isn't me. You have not done anything wrong here, but I need to do what's best for me.

That's why I have gone. I'm going back to the UK. I've spoken to Helena and told her. I'm leaving immediately so will probably already be in the air by the time you read this.

I meant what I said Nicholas. Your happiness is more important than my broken heart. I want you and Castor to be happy. Please be happy.

I think now that I know you are finally going to be with your person, I think I can move on. I just can't do that here.

I'm sorry.

I love you Nicholas.

Yours, Milo

CHAPTER 7.

Milo

I pay the driver and step out of the hackney cab, lugging my large rucksack, loaded with as much essential stuff as I could grab from my room at the resort. I still had a large amount of stuff back in Crete. I figure that if it feels right being back at home I can send for my stuff, or pout until Gio goes for me. I open the small waist-high wrought iron gate and traverse the narrow path, encroached upon by the overflowing border plants that my mother says makes this house a home. Strange, because I've always thought that people made the house a home; turns out it's honeysuckle and hellebore plants.

The white net curtains hanging inside the living room of my parents' house begin to twitch, the sound of the gate alerting my dad of either visitors, postmen or potential invaders. A moment later the entire net curtain is lifted away from the large bay window at the front of the house. My mother and father's joyful smiling faces are pressed up against the glass like prisoners from the Midnight Express.

"I don't have my key," I mouth at them. It's a strange social construct that if someone is a few feet from you it's okay to shout, whereas if there is a pane of glass between you, you are socially obligated to speak in muted tones and mouth your communication.

My mother's hands ball around each other and come to her chest, and she nods and beams a smile at me. The curtain drops as I hear the sounds of her delighted squeals as she trots down the hallway towards the door. The door flies open, banging against the wall just inside. I see my dad wince, no doubt calculating how much he will be spending at B&Q come the weekend to patch that dent.

"Oh lord, what are you doing here?" My mother rushes towards me, wrapping her arms around me and pulling me into a tight embrace. I drop my rucksack and return her hug, smelling the familiar sweet jasmine of her perfume. The tight coil of anxiety and pain that has been lodged in my gut loosens a fraction at the scent of home.

"Can I not just come and see my parents?" I wink at my dad over her shoulder.

"Oh no," my dad sighs, "did Nicholas finally fire you? What could you have done to get fired, son?"

"He didn't fire me Dad," I laugh. "I just think maybe it's not the right place for me anymore."

My mother pulls back from the hug and drags me into the house. We settle in the living room, and I choose to sit on one of her oversized and overstuffed floral armchairs with the problem patterns that she seems to love so much. "So does this mean you are coming home for good?" she smiles at me hopefully.

"Maybe" I shrug, "would that be okay?"

"This is your home as much as ours my boy," my father grins.

The sound of the front door slamming closed startles me. My head snaps to the doorway as my brother walks into the room, nodding at each of our parents. His gaze settles on me as his mouth sags open. "What the fuck are you doing here?" he gasps.

Reaching forward, my dad whacks Gio on the back of the head with a rolled-up newspaper. "Show some respect," he barks, "there are ladies present." My mother preens at him before offering Gio a seat next to her on the sofa.

"So?" He gestures towards me.

All three of them stare at me like I am about to offer them some giant revelation or profound reason for sitting amongst them. "I just came home," I shrug. "I missed England and I think I'm finally done with Crete." I fiddle with the bag straps of my bag which lies between my feet.

"Nice," Gio smiles, "this calls for a celebration. Milo, can you give me a hand in the kitchen to bring some glasses in please? I'm going to open some wine," he says to my mother who smiles and asks for a nice Pinot.

The kitchen door closes quietly behind Gio. I open the cupboard and pluck out four wine glasses. "Cut the shit," my brother barks, standing close behind me. I fumble the glasses in my hand and barely manage to stop them from falling to the stone floor where they would surely smash into smithereens.

"What?" I snap petulantly.

"What are you doing here?" He lays a hand on my shoulder. "And you can leave out the lovey-dovey *I just want to be home* spiel, because I don't buy it."

"Gio I just…"

"Milo." Gio pins me with a stare. The stare that I know brooks no bullshit of any variety.

I take a deep breath in. "It's just not the right fit for me anymore," I shrug, rinsing out the glasses in the sink. "Nicholas doesn't need me there anymore. I have learned what I need to learn and now I can move on. Anyways,

Castor is moving back in with him so it will be quite crowded."

"And there it is," Gio smiles.

"There what is?" I shake my head as if I have no idea what he is talking about.

"You are far too transparent Milo." Gio squeezes my shoulder. "You have always been far too transparent when it comes to Nick. You used to follow us around all the time making moon eyes at him. I thought as you got older that you would be able to deal with your crush on him, but it just seemed to get worse with every year."

"Oh god," I gasp, "was I really that bad? Did Nicholas think I was a little stalker who wouldn't leave him alone? No wonder he is always pissed at me."

"On the contrary." Gio shook his head slightly. "It got to a point where Nicholas kept on looking at you in the same way too. I tried to keep you two apart as much as I could because it was so fucking weird, but eventually I gave in. I figured if I could get you a job there with Nicholas, you would both pull your heads out your arseholes and maybe something would happen."

"You what?" My mouth gapes open.

"I'm sorry Milo." My brother pulls me into a hug. "If Nick doesn't see what a catch you are, then it's his fucking loss."

My breath hitches in my throat as I choke back a sob, the feelings and frustration that have been building since this morning begging to be freed. I squeeze my brother before pulling back. "Listen Gio." I wipe my cheek. "I don't really feel in the mood to celebrate anything now. I'm going to sneak upstairs and try to sleep. Can you tell Mum and Dad

I'm sorry, and I will be in a much better mood tomorrow? It's been a long day."

"Go get your head down bro," he smiles, carrying the glasses and wine into the living room.

I make it upstairs without being accosted and fall face-first onto the bed in the far guestroom. I press my face into the cool pillow and close my eyes. In only a few minutes pain and exhaustion win out, and I let sleep claim me.

CHAPTER 8.

Milo

A few hours later a heavy persistent knocking against the door pulls me from a deep sleep. I groan, pulling the pillow over my head. "Go away," I moan through the door, "people are trying to sleep." I feel myself drifting off, the mattress and the soft sheets pulling me back into my slumber. Then another round of irritating intrusive knocking shatters the last remnants of my dream. I swing my legs off the bed and stumble towards the door, fully intending to give whoever is on the other side of the door a piece of my mind. I would have to apologise later. Ballbust first, sorry after.

I whip the door open. "What do you thi…" is all I get out. Standing on the other side of the door, looking exhausted but slightly relieved, is Nicholas. I rub at my eyes. "I must still be dreaming."

"No, definitely not dreaming," Nicholas breathes. "Can I come in?"

I stand there, mouth open and gaping as I nod slightly and step aside. Nicholas brushes past me, his fingertips grazing over my wrist as he passes. The warm scent of spices and oranges cling to his skin. The scent of the resort lingers on him, even thousands of miles away. I close the door and rest my forehead against the cool wooden surface of the door. *What on earth is he doing here?*

"So…" he starts, and I turn to face him. "You're here."

"Yeah I am." *Well this is some stellar conversation we are having at the moment.*

"Do you maybe want to tell me why?" He catches the corner of his top lip between his teeth.

"I don't know," I shrug, "I don't think I belong there anymore."

"What do you mean?" A deep wrinkle appears on his brow. It looks kind of adorable, so much so that I want to go to him and smooth it out with my thumb. "Of course you belong there."

"Why?" I take a step towards him. "It's not as if I make much of a difference there, only to annoy you, flirt with the guests and keep Lana company," I joke. I do a lot at the resort and he knows it. I'm the only one who can manage the complicated rota and keep everyone happy. Without me there, someone is going to have to play peacemaker to stop civil war from breaking out. I'm also the only person whom George from the drinks vendors will give his company discount. It helps to be adorable.

"You do a lot more than that," he whispers. "You mean a lot to us at the resort."

"Thanks Boss." I chuckle sadly. Just what a boy wants to hear from his crush, that he is a very valuable asset to the organisation.

"You know that's not what I meant." Nicholas moves to take a seat at the edge of my bed and taps the space next to him. I frown and take a tentative step towards him. I sit down gingerly beside him, my hands clasped tightly on my lap in front of me. "You mean a lot to me. I don't want you to go."

"Nicholas…"

"No, please let me finish. I've not been fair to you for quite a while now. I let my own issues get in the way of how I should be treating you. I thought it was the only way to keep things okay between us." I have no idea what it is he is trying to say, but judging by the way he's grinding his teeth, neither does he.

"I'm really confused, Nicholas."

Slowly but surely, he reaches across and grabs my hand, linking his fingers with mine. My breath hitches at the contact. "Then let me be really clear. I'm so into you, Milo. I know that's weird cause I'm your brother's friend and I'm so much older, and I know that I shouldn't have these feelings about you, but I do. I have tried so hard not to have them, but I can't seem to stop. That's why I am always such an arse with you at work. I figure if I can't grab you and kiss you like I want to do every damn time I lay eyes on you, then the only way is to stay away from you and that means being an arsehole. That doesn't make much sense right now to me either, but it did back then."

"What!" I bark.

"I know. I'm so sorry. Please, though, you don't have to leave because of the way I act toward you. I can keep my feelings in check and do better by you. I mean I'm likely going to have a bit of an issue when I see you flirting with other guys, hence this," he laughs, raising his cast in front of his face.

"What do you mean?"

"I saw you flirting with that guy at the bar. I watched you from the window and I got so jealous. Next thing I knew, my fist was through the wall and Helena was telling me how much of an idiot I was." I cover my mouth with my hand to stop from laughing, but I can totally picture Helena yelling at him, whilst his fist was pouring blood. She would have made a great battlefield sergeant.

"You were jealous? Over me?" *This can't be happening, right?*

"Of course I was. Milo, I have wanted you ever since that night at your birthday party. Something changed for me that night, and it never went back to the way it was. My need for you only got stronger." His uninjured hand squeezes my own.

It's only then that the handsome doctor appears unbidden in my thoughts. "What about Castor?"

Nicholas frowns, before a small smile appears on his mouth. "What about him?"

"He said you two were getting back together." I try to slip my hand from his. He only squeezes mine tighter, holding me in place, which I have no real problem with

"Milo, listen to me. I am not getting back together with Castor. I'm not getting together with anyone. It would be unfair of me to date someone right now?" My heart slowly fills with cautious joy.

"Why?"

"Because it's not fair to start dating someone when I'm very clearly in love with someone else." A small look of hope flits across his expression.

"You love me?" I can't contain the smile that spreads across my face.

"I know it's super fast, but I've also known you forever so it feels like it's been a long time coming. The second I read your letter I knew I couldn't let you go. I won't let you go without a fight Milo. I want us to give this a go; do you?"

I could say a lot of things in that moment. I could say that I've wanted him for as long as I could remember. I could say that he's everything I've ever wanted but never knew I could have. I could say that I've loved him before I even knew what love was. I don't say any of that though. I simply pull him towards me, my arms going up around his neck as I pull his mouth down against mine.

We kiss gently and slowly for what seems like hours, his tongue dancing and sliding against mine. This isn't the passionate tearing off of clothes that the movies would have us believe, this is the culmination of years of love and affection finally finding its release. I know his heart races and matches my own. He smiles against my lips, the happiness evident on his face.

"You know your brother might kill me, right?" he mumbles against my mouth.

"I think you'll find he will be more than okay with this," I grin back.

"Come home with me," he whispers.

Home.

I smile.

The End

ABOUT THE AUTHOR

J S Grey lives in Warrington, North West England with his husband, son, and Black Labrador. Having always wanted to write M/M romance, he spends his time reading M/M romance novels and watching awful TV shows he secretly loves.

To learn more visit:

Facebook - https://www.facebook.com/AuthorJSGrey/

Instagram - https://www.instagram.com/thejsgrey/?hl=en

Website - http://www.thejsgrey.com

Other Books by JS Grey

Consuming Redemption – Love in the North *(Book 1 in the Four Corners Series)*

Raven's Way – *(Takes places within the Four Corners Universe)*

All books can be read as standalone Novels.

Chapter 1

Michael

2002

I stare out of the passenger window watching as parents herd their children along cramped pavements, aiming for the schools at the end of the long busy high street, trying to dodge the onslaught of walking commuters as they make their way, heads dipped, hoods up, earphones firmly jammed in their ears, towards whichever office desk beckons them. I can relate to their hesitance in reaching their destination; I would rather be headed anywhere else than the high school I was headed for.

Icy rain pelts against the windshield of my brother's 2001 sea-green Vauxhall Corsa. The wiper blades work overtime swiping away the frosty deluge pouring from a dark sky. The narcissist in me almost believes the gloomy atmosphere is a reflection of my current mood.

"How long are you going to be in jail for?" my brother Caleb mutters from the driver's seat next to me, his eyes never straying from the road.

"Jail?" My eyebrows furrow as I struggle to grasp what the hell he's talking about.

"I assumed from your face and general pissy attitude that you must be getting locked away today and not just going to school."

I pull the hood of my black wool peacoat up around my head, flipping him off in the process. I reach into the pocket of my coat, pulling out my iPod, tucking the earphones into my ears. I feel a hand at my face as my brother reaches across to yank the cables free.

"Hey, dick!" I yelp as the buds are pulled harshly away from my ears. My index fingers smooth away the slight sting from the sudden ejection. I reach across and give him a firm punch in the bicep. Caleb had played rugby for the school before graduating last year. He still has the body of a quality fullback, his forearms moulded strong through years of practice. The fullback is the last line of defence in any major play in rugby. My brother had been the star of our family - my parents never missed a game or failed to tell all of their friends at the golf club about their rugby star son. *He's going all the way to the top,* my dad would croon whenever he got a chance.

"Seriously what the fuck is wrong with you?" The corners of Caleb's eyes crease in apparent concern. At that moment something catches my attention as we pull up at the gates of the high school. I see the olive green fur-hooded parka belonging to *what the fuck is wrong with me.* I watch as he walks amongst his minions through tall wrought iron gates set between high spiked railings. A cold sensation unfurls in my gut as I begin to imagine the laundry list of possible annoyances he and his cronies will throw my way today.

I turn back towards my brother and try for a toothy smile, but the wince on my brother's face indicates it hasn't achieved the result I was intending. "What?" I go for a shrug, hoping the nonchalance will make him believe I don't give a fuck.

"What are you doing with your face?" he says, his eyebrows rising.

"I'm smiling at you?" I hate the fact that he can read me like an open book.

"That's not a smile Michael, you're showing me your teeth like a psychopath. You're smiling at me like Paulette from *Legally Blonde*."

The corners of my mouth lift in a shit-eating grin. "Legally Blonde?" I clicked my tongue on the inside of my cheek, "I thought I was the gay one in the family?"

Something passes over Caleb's expression, which has me bringing my internal walls back up, cutting me off from whatever brotherly bonding session I think we might currently be having. I'd forgotten for a moment the unspoken rule that I don't talk about my sexuality. Whereas Caleb was the star rugby player of the family, I'm the disgraced former star footballer. You might be thinking I quit due to injury, or by my grades being so low that the 'Coach wouldn't let me play. No, I'd mistakenly believed I was living in a more accepting time, so I didn't spend too long deciding that on my 15th birthday last June, I would tell all of my loyal friends and loving family that I was gay. Yeah, turns out, not so *loyal* or *loving*.

"So..." Caleb sputters out, his voice, high-pitched. I can almost see the gears cranking around in his head as he scrambles for a quick change of topic. "What did you have planned for today?" he spits out finally.

"Erm... School?" I say, gesturing out of the window with my thumb. Caleb looks around the car awkwardly like he has lost something. Wanting to give him an out, I unbuckle my seatbelt and reach for my dark navy blue backpack on the back seat.

"Do you need me to pick you up tonight?" The offer seems empty like he is hoping I will say no. "I have a date later on this evening, but I can swing back after work and collect you."

"A date huh?" I laugh, turning back to face him. Caleb's cheeks redden, which I think has nothing to do with the warm air currently blowing from the fans on the dashboard.

"Yeah, just someone I met recently; I don't think it's serious. I mean she says she isn't looking for anything serious." His gaze drops slightly which startles me; Caleb has always been a 'love the one you're with' kinda guy, as long as the one you're with' didn't mind that you didn't do repeats.

"Is that what you want?" I watch a dozen emotions play out over his face as if he's trying to find the answer within himself.

"I don't know. I mean she is nice. I think mum and dad would love her." I roll my eyes. "What?"

"Caleb, mum, and dad will love anyone you bring back. You're their light at the end of the tunnel."

Caleb's eyes widen in surprise. "What's that supposed to mean?"

"You're their key to forever: they see their grandchildren in your future. If you bring them home a nice girl then they are going to be the happiest they have been in a while. They're proud of you."

His hand comes to rest on my shoulder as I train my eyes on the floor mats. "Michael, they're proud of you too," he insists, his hand squeezing briefly.

"Yeah until I bring home someone I like."

His hand stills on my shoulder and he takes in a deep breath. It's not in him to lie to me, so he says nothing.

"Do you know that they told me? That I was just trying to get attention when my teacher Mrs. Berry called them a few weeks ago."

"Yes, but weren't you doing some protest monologue in health class?"

I huff out a sigh. "No, I was merely educating Mrs. Berry that when she talked about the 'Normal Family'," I say making quotation signs with my fingers, "that normal could mean lots of different things to different people. I just asked her when I married my husband, would that make it abnormal?"

My brother smiles sadly, "But two men can't get married, Michael."

I grit my teeth, my fingers curling around the straps of my bag. "I know that! It won't be that way forever though." *I bloody well hope not.*

"Maybe just try and be a little less...you know," Caleb says, wiggling his hand from side to side like I'm some kind of codebreaker who will just get what he is talking about.

"No, a little less what?" I stare pointedly at him.

"You know, a little less in your face about certain things," he says, his voice soft as if trying to appease an idiot, "a little less you."

I don't think it would have hurt more if he had physically punched me in the stomach. Whilst it isn't something we discuss openly, I had always assumed that Caleb has my back and accepts me. Yet, it turns out he thinks I'm some flaming homo who just needs to calm down. My stomach feels hollow; I can feel the last tenuous links to my family slipping away before my eyes and I'm powerless to stop it.

I quickly smile and nod at him, not able to spend one more minute in the car with him.

"Are you sure I can't pick you up tonight?" he murmurs.

I shake my head and reach to open the door, the cold metal of the handle hard against my fingers. I have to force myself to make my hand move, instinct telling me just to go home and go back to bed and forget about today already.

"Later bro." I hear the soft voice behind me, and the cold rage inching its way through my veins forces me to open the door and push myself out into the rain.

Other work by JS Grey

Consuming Redemption: Love in the North

CHAPTER ONE

Tyler

2001

The shrill sound of my alarm screeches next to my bed. The sharp chill of winter bites in the air; my mother, always trying to be as green as possible shuts off the heating last thing at night. The covers, still pulled over my head, only dull the sound slightly. I know I have moments before my mother, in her booming voice, starts telling me to shut the damn thing off.

I reach out from underneath the blankets, the frigid air raising goosebumps along the length of my arm. As I now have this practiced down to a fine art, I'm able to take one quick swipe at the gold-coloured bell alarm that adorns my bedside table, knocking the thing under my bed and silencing the demon device. The quiet gives me the moments of peace I need to fall back into a dreamless sleep. I pull the blankets back over my head and snuggle into their delicious warmth.

"Don't even think of going back to sleep Tyler!" my mother calls from the next room.

"I'm not!" I yell back through the wall.

"Then why are the covers back over your head?" I pull down my duvet looking around to see if somehow she has managed to creep into my room unnoticed. Seeing I'm alone in my room, I frown at the wall.

"That's better," she calls. My eyes widen as I stare at the adjoining wall.

"Gotta be a witch," I mutter to myself. Swinging my legs off the side of the bed I give myself a moment to contemplate existence as I stare into the middle distance, my brain now fully awake.

Suddenly the realisation hits me: "It's not Saturday, it's Friday!" I groan, falling back onto the bed. Another day at that god-damned place before the sweet precious release of the weekend.

The weekend is a place of solitude and peace where I can be whoever the hell I want to be without the constant worry that I'm going to run into *him*. School would be fairly enjoyable if it wasn't for *him*. I get along well with most of my teachers, and when I am given the time and space to concentrate during class I get good grades. All of that changed though the day Lukas Ford came into my life.

Forcing myself to stand, I stumble past the discarded clothes I had left on the floor the night before and head towards my bathroom. I stop along the way to open the dark wooden slats currently blocking the rising sun's rays from entering my room. Flicking on the bathroom light, I rub away the remnants of slumber from my eyes and gaze at myself in the mirror. The thick blonde neck-length hair that normally falls quite nicely and frames my face has rearranged itself into quite a decent-looking bird's nest on top of my head. I run my long fingers through the messy mop, before resigning myself to the fact that I'm going to have to wash and dry it into some type of style. I give myself an appraising once-over. My light blue eyes stare back at me tiredly, the threat of dark circles under my eyes trying to make themselves known on my slightly tanned complexion.

There were times when my self esteem was affected not only by *him,* but by what I perceived to be the shallowness of my own thoughts. I had looked at myself in this very mirror previously and thought to myself, *But I'm actually quite hot, shouldn't I be popular?,* before giving myself an internal bitch slap for sounding like a dick. Shallow me wasn't wrong though, I am not a bad guy to look at: nice full lips, a dimpled chin that reminded me of Clark Kent from old Superman comics, sunkissed skin that gave the impression that I had either spent a lot of dedicated hours at the beach, or had made regular visits to the sunbed, when in fact I had my mother's Italian heritage to thank for my naturally olive skin.

Whilst our surname might be Dane through my father's side, my mother's original surname had been Fiorentino, which I thought was just awesome. She had not been convinced when I had begun high school to let me use her maiden name instead of my father's name. So I'm just plain old Tyler Dane.

After taking a quick shower and pulling on what I think will be acceptable wallflower attire I make my way downstairs. My mother has beaten me to it; she's standing at the stovetop pouring pancake batter and blueberries into a skillet.

"I'm going out on a limb and saying I think it's a pancake kind of morning," she says, craning her neck around the corner to give me a small wink.

I hand her a small dish and nod. "Load me up please; that bacon as well," I say, pointing to the stack of crispy streaky bacon piled on a greasy kitchen towel next to her. Letting out a small breathy chuckle she nods and puts a few rashers on the plate. "Syrup?" I ask in a more accusatory tone. She purses her lips and reaches onto the shelf next to the stovetop, pulling down a small white jar of maple syrup. Pouring on what could arguably be called a drip onto my plate, she hands it to me. I move across to a small dining nook on the far side of the room and take a seat at our old country style farm table.

"Your teeth are going to fall out you know?" she tells me matter-of-factly, "Also it's really not fair how you can eat that much food and still stay in shape."

"Curse of all this beauty," I say, gesturing from my face down my body with a flourish of my hand. My mother smiles wide and nods.

"So what's the plan for today?" she asks.

My mood sours almost immediately. She picks the paper up from the worktop and comes to join me at the table, taking a seat on the bench opposite me. The gleam in her eye fills me with a morose sadness, she is likely hoping against hope that I've sprung some kind of social life overnight and that I'll tell her I'm going to a party or meeting some friends and getting drunk in a park somewhere.

"Just school then home." I try for a bright smile, but from the look she gives me I can see she isn't buying whatever it is I'm trying to sell her.

"My handsome boy, I know things aren't great right now, but I promise you, just hold on and things will get better." She reaches across the old wooden table and rests her hand over mine.

"They have to," I smile. She bites her bottom lip and looks down at the paper, the pain tangible on her face. "I'll be ok, but only if I get going now otherwise I'm going to be late," I say, glancing down at my watch. My mother loves me, of this I am very sure, but part of me hates myself for making her worry about me. I wish I could be normal like everyone else and not weigh her down with the burden of having me for a son. Running back up to my room, I grab the last of my things and head out the door towards school.

Six hours after I arrive at school I stare out of the classroom window, watching the icy rain pelt against the windowpane. The clouds were already dark, growing thicker with each passing hour. The noise of the water hitting the glass distracts me from listening to our History teacher trying desperately to make the Industrial Revolution interesting to a group of 16-year-old high schoolers on a Friday afternoon. The battle had been lost before it had begun; she knows it, the students know it, but pretenses must be kept up. So, on the lesson goes.

"Can anyone tell me firstly, what a Spinning Jenny is, and secondly, how its invention is mirrored in automation today?" Miss Allen stares out at the sea of blank faces, I glance around at the looks of confusion on the faces of the other students as they suddenly realise that they have been asked a direct question. "Does anyone need me to repeat the question?"

I stare around the classroom, looking from person to person in hopes that one of them had the answer stored somewhere in their subconscious. I know from experience that if someone doesn't come up with an answer fast then Miss Allen will 'call upon someone at random', *meaning she will ask me directly,* for the answer. Gazes avert to the floor, the ceiling, out of the window, staring desperately at the person's head in front of them... anywhere but directly at Miss Allen.

"Any takers?" I can already feel her eyes searching the classroom for me before she finishes asking her last question. "Ah, Mr. Dane, would you care to enlighten us as to the use of the Spinning Jenny?"

I can feel the tension leave the rest of the students around me, and the clear joy at not being asked the dreaded 'gotcha' question. Their lizard brains seem to wake up though, noticing that the socially weakest among them has been highlighted for the kill. Whispers shoot up around the classroom.

My brain quickly tries to access the stored knowledge that I know is hidden somewhere in there. We had talked about this in the last session. Something about....GAH! The correct answer hovers on the periphery of my brain but refuses to come clearly into the light of day. Each time I think of the phrase 'Spinning Jenny', my brain becomes very adolescent and thinks of most perverse answers. I look to Miss Allen desperately, my eyes pleading for a reprieve, one which I know will not come. Miss Allen smiles at me, waiting for my response to her ridiculous question posed at 2pm Friday. Does she not know school finishes in two hours? What is the reason for this torture... education, that's it.

Suddenly the fog lifts, and my brain lights up and has a *eureka* moment. "I think the Spinning Jenny was a multi-spindle spinning frame?" My eyes shoot down to the table immediately, hoping to miss the disappointment on my History teacher's face or the looks of vicarious embarrassment surely plastered on my classmates' faces. The answer suddenly seems not so correct in my head.

"Thank god one of you actually pays attention. You all could learn something from Mr. Dane here. You don't have to go out partying every weekend to have a good time, sometimes the quest for knowledge can be just as exhilarating!" I wonder how long it would take for me to will myself to burst into a ball of flames to destroy all evidence of my body and my shame. My face is surely hot enough to make this happen.

I feel the heated glare of people staring at me with a mixture of pity and hatred. I am by no stretch of the imagination popular. Actually, that's incorrect; if by being the go-to guy for someone to beat up, or dump their lunch or drink over, or shove into the bushes, then I am definitely very popular. Being the only confirmed gay guy in a high school in the North of England will generally have that effect.

I have never openly admitted to my classmates that I was gay, but it's clear for the world to see. My thin frame, clad in skinny jeans and colorful graphic t-shirts confirms everyone's suspicions. Given that every other male 16-year-old in the school wears solely track suits and sneakers, the one kid daring to wear something other than the socially approved attire means only one thing to these guys... gay.

I've known I was different from the first time I watched Interview with the Vampire and Brad Pitt had exploded my world. The feast of flesh on screen from the many beautiful female actors had not once prized my view from Louis the Vampire: his long dirty blonde hair, the full pouting lips and those broad perfect pecs. Maybe the term gay hadn't felt right at that point, but I had known then that something was different about me.

"Would you like to inform your classmates why the Spinning Jenny mirrors the issues with automation and workforce issues today?" She asks the question with a certain smugness to her voice. It is the type of smugness that comes from being sure that later in the day, you will not get your ass kicked. I can make myself no such promises.

Teachers have been my armour since I came to realise that I am at the very bottom rung of the social hierarchy in high school. Scratch that, I'm one of the little plastic things at the bottom of the stubby legs of the ladder. Teachers have provided a type of safe haven for my mind when my thoughts turn dark to the fact that my classmates are basically unaware of my existence, and when they become aware it is only to brush past me, shove me out their way or to kick my ass for daring to exist in their presence. I can tell myself that at least the teachers see me, that they value me as a human being and that I am worth more than the others lead me to believe. This time however I wish Miss Allen had also glossed over my existence.

Part of me at that moment hates her, but my conscience will not allow that to happen for long. A crushing guilt settles into the pit of my stomach as I see the look of pride on her face as I realise how much she enjoys having me there. She deserves to have at least one person in the class give an actual fuck rather than some mumbled response designed to placate her and move her along to the next topic.

"At the time of its invention, it enabled fibers to be spun at the same rate of eight workers, which allowed for the faster production of coarse fiber materials. Also, as the invention became more popular, cloth was imported at a much cheaper price than that produced more locally in England. So not only had the machine cut the workforce requirement, but the labor was being outsourced to India and China." I barely take a breath as I speak, to get the word vomit out as quickly as possible. No sooner has the answer left my mouth than a voice sounds from the back of class, sending a thrill snaking down my spine, exciting and terrifying me in equal measure.

"Of course, teacher's little faggot got the answer right, probably spent last night having a sleepover with Teach, huh Tyler?" I know that voice like I know my own. It is *him.*

I turn to face Lukas Ford like some kind of homing pigeon: I hear his voice and my eyes gravitate towards him. This pigeon however is like a bird with a crack habit - no matter how much I know making myself visible to him makes me his target, I can't seem to help myself.

I think back to that first day when Lukas Ford moved to our town and my high school.

I had been lost in my own thoughts running a paintbrush across a canvas on the easel in front of me, trying to find a way to alter a classical piece of artwork into something more contemporary and coming up blank. I had hoped that if I just started working, inspiration would strike. I hadn't looked up when the classroom door had opened, or even when Mrs. Woods, the Art teacher, introduced the new student Lukas to the entire class. Lost in my thoughts, my head snapped up when I heard her voice speak to me directly.

"Did you hear what I said Tyler? Can you please show Lukas where to get an easel, canvas and supplies?" She looked at me the same way a quizzical Labrador would look at its master doing a handstand, with a tilted head and furrowed brow. I only saw Mrs. Woods however.

"Who?" She motioned her head to the side with a nod to her right. There is no one standing next to her.

She frowned and threw up her hands. "To your left Tyler, I swear it's like you live on a different planet sometimes."

I suddenly became aware of a presence beside me. My head snapped to the side and I gave a startled yelp. A quick laugh escaped the boy standing next to me. My eyes struggled to process him. He was a LOT! I allowed myself a precious second for my eyes to roam over the Greek god in front of me, or what passed for a Greek god to the eyes of a kid who was twelve years old.

The first thing I noticed were the honey coloured eyes giving me a curious stare, as if I'd asked a question he was struggling to answer. I took in his dark brown hair, thick and shiny, cropped short at the sides but with a mess of curls on the top that you could only get away with if you knew you were cool. I fisted my hands at my sides to stop myself from running my fingers through his hair. My eyes settled on Lukas's full mouth with (oh god) a full, pouty bottom lip...

"Erm....hello? Aaaaaanybody home?" I suddenly realised that like a creeper, I had been staring and obviously perusing the new kid in class in full view of the rest of my classmates, while he was waving his hand in front of my face and biting back a smile. "I think you are supposed to be helping me here man. I don't know where anything is."

My brain sputtered back to life and I finally drew in a sharp breath. I knew I had to say something, anything. But nothing seemed to be coming out of my mouth. I prayed something would come out – anything would be better than this dead air

*currently crackling around us. Suddenly I had it! "You're new."
Well done, genius. I squinted my eyes and thought that I
probably shouldn't have said anything.*

*"Yep, that's right, like I said I don't know where anything is,
could you show me where to get set up?" Again this was a
normal request which should have elicited a normal response,
but there was nothing normal about what was happening to my
brain right now. Under normal circumstances I would have
assumed I was suffering from some form of obscure neurological
disorder that removed IQ points from the victim at a rapid pace.*

*My breathing started to pick up, I was inhaling way too much
air, and a full blown panic attack was definitely on the horizon.
Before I had a chance to mutter back a half-assed response,
which was what I was sure what was coming next, my world
came crashing down around me.*

*"Hey check it out, gay boy is popping a boner over the new kid!"
I looked around wondering who the hell was shouting and who
they were shouting about. I saw Caleb Irwin was pointing
directly at me and laughing, tears streaming down his face. I
looked down at myself and sure enough I was starting to tent
inside my trousers. The protrusion was pointing directly at the
new kid as if to blame him for daring to awaken it. Heat filled
my cheeks once more and I moved to cover myself. I looked up
at him in hopes that I wouldn't see the disgust that I ultimately
expected to see there. His face twisted into a mean scowl as he
looked around the room as if to let everyone else know that he
was not a part of this.*

*Caleb stalked up behind me and whispered into his ear, "I don't
think he wants what you're offering, faggot." The sneering tone
of his words dripped into my mind and settled down in my
stomach making it churn to the point where I felt as if I would*

throw up the contents of my lunch. Caleb reached around me and patted Lukas on the shoulder. "Come on man, I'll show you where to get set up. I think if this homo takes you into the store room he might try to suck your dick or something."

Lukas chuckled at Caleb and moved quickly away from me. The simple move felt like a sword piercing my stomach, letting all the shame pool on the floor for all to see. Each and every person in the room was reacting to the sight in their own way. Some were laughing directly in my face, some were muttering words of disgust and some were sporting scowls of anger and frustration that they could not react violently towards me as there was a person of authority in the room.

"Thanks man, yeah I definitely do not swing that way," Lukas laughed and looked over his shoulder at me. His eyes narrowed before he turned back towards Caleb.

Mrs. Woods had stayed oddly quiet throughout the incident, her eyes darting around the classroom at anyone but me. Finally she let out a resigned sigh and came up beside me. "Maybe you might feel more comfortable skipping the rest of this lesson and doing some studying for your SATs in the library." Her hand came to rest gingerly on my shoulder. "Best not to disturb the rest of the class, don't you agree?"

I couldn't believe what I was hearing; rather than reprimand the class for their obvious discriminatory behavior, she was penalizing me and ejecting me from the classroom like some deviant. I sank my chin to my chest and quickly gathered my things, hearing the muttering of people around me. I knew it was a matter of time before word spread around the school about me, and stories tended to become skewed until they were far worse than the actual event. Once packed, I slung my backpack over my shoulder and hurried from the classroom, *making my way quickly to the admissions office to request a change out of Art class. I couldn't protect myself from the eventual onslaught from the school, but I could make sure I would never have to go back to that classroom.*

Printed in Great Britain
by Amazon